The Will of Joan Goode 1793

Julius Falconer

Eloquent Books
New York, New York

Eloquent Book Publishing
An imprint of Writers Literary & Publishing Services, Inc.
845 Third Avenue, 6th Floor–6016
New York, NY 10022
http://www.strategicbookpublishing.com

ISBN: 978-1-60860-158-5

Printed in the United States of America

Book Design/Layout by: Andrew Herzog

This book is dedicated to
Catherine and Jeffrey
with gratitude and deep affection

He is a fool who thinks by might or skill
To force the current of a woman's will.

Sir Samuel Tuke (c.1615-1674)
Adventures of Five Hours, Act V, scene 3

Foreword

The Will which lies at the heart of this story, given in full in chapter II, is a genuine will, readily available in a public collection in the United Kingdom. A few short phrases have been added or omitted, and names of people and places have been changed to protect the living. Otherwise it–and the codicils–stand as originally written. The family history behind the Will, detailed in chapter VII, is also substantially historical and has been researched from original documents. For the rest, I cannot stress too strongly that this is a work of fiction and that no persons mentioned in the text have any relation whatever to real people living or dead, except in my imagination.

J.F.

I

A Demd, Damp, Moist, Unpleasant Body!
Charles Dickens, Nicholas Nickleby, Chapter 34

The snow fell steadily, casting a white sheet over the houses and fields that constituted the picturesque village of Halton Thoresby. The small copses were silent as even the birds that made themselves visible in an English winter retreated to roosts and perches to keep warm. The lanes that connected the village to two main roads had filled with snow, so little traffic was there this Christmas Eve. Coils of smoke wound up into the sullen sky from chimneys Jacobean and Victorian, from cottage and manor, from inn and villa. Street-lights shed a somewhat garish glare across the falling snow-flakes. The village green, round an ancient chestnut, shone dully white in the gleam from windows of those few cottagers who had not yet closed their curtains against the bitter night. Not even those who yearned for a white Christmas could have dreamt of anything quite so perfect. Mrs Vickers, in her double-fronted house down a side lane off the village green, surrounded by its own garden and attached to the lane by a winding path edged in summer with lavender, could not imagine a better night on which to welcome the Savior, and she looked forward to the midnight service which followed Mr and Mrs Vickers' annual Christmas soirée for their friends in the village.

Guests were already on their way, wrapped up to ward off the cold, and appropriately shod with spare shoes in a bag in their hand. They walked as quickly as the snow would allow, careful not to slip but anxious to reach the haven of Anchor Lodge, where they knew warmth, good food and pleasant company awaited them. All the guests were long-standing friends, or at least acquaintances, used to greeting each other in the village store or in the church–those who attended!–or at other social venues of Halton Thorseby like the pub, the bowling-green and the tennis club. Halton Thoresby did not boast a library, or a second shop, much less anything so coarse as a cinema or bingo hall. (The very idea!) The Vickers' annual soirée was welcomed in a special way, not only because of its inherent good cheer but also because it marked the imminent approach of Christmas in the village–the ideal prelude to the church service which they knew the vicar, old Mr Thew, would conduct with discretion: a few decently short hymns, a short sermon, and a spiritual uplift as he bade them go carefully into the night.

First amongst the guests to arrive were Dr and Mrs Wartenby Simpson, general practitioner, and his wife of forty years. They lived on the edge of the village, in a suitably upbeat house, which they had bought a year or two ago in preparation for the doctor's retirement (from Cannington, the nearest town, home to 3000 souls, in which he has labored for thirty-five years) and which they kept trim and painted to promote the image they wished to project. Wartenby was the dominant partner in the team, but it was their daughter rather than their son who had inherited the overbearing manner.

Shortly behind them came the Matthewsons, husband and wife. Julius practiced as a solicitor in Bolham, the town in the opposite direction to Cannington, where he had gained a reputation for being a canny operator. His wife Deirdre, on the other hand, was very active in village life: the WI, the church, the bowling club, the social whirl. Their house on the village green almost rivaled the manor in grandeur, with elaborate gates, tall chimneys and a general air of prosperity. The lawns swept down towards the gates, the trees rose high into the sky, the perimeter wall was immaculately free of vegetable growths. To their disappointment, they were childless, but two Irish wolfhounds were some sort of substitute. Mr and Mrs Matthewson were accompanied by a friend of theirs from the Home Counties, a certain Thornton Dismore who had been invited to stay for Christmas because his nephew Simeon and his wife, with whom he normally spent the festivities, had decided this year to go for a cruise to the Maldives. Thornton was something in banking–the Matthewsons never seemed to find out exactly what–a widower of about forty with few interests seemingly outside a passion for French châteaux and the television. The Vickerses had readily agreed to welcome the Matthewsons' guest as their own–'the spirit of Christmas and all that', Sally Vickers had intoned.

After the Matthewsons, almost on their heels, arrived the only bachelor of the party, a certain Martin Gee, with whom we become acquainted only to discover that he passes rapidly–and one must suppose reluctantly–out of our story (and indeed out of life altogether). Martin, or Mr Gee as he would perhaps prefer us to call him, was a pernickety individual whose failure to attract a mate was readily comprehensible to most impartial observers of human nature. He dressed fussily, walked with a mincing gait and spoke in orotund fashion. He was, however, a ready conversationalist and could be guaranteed to keep conversation moving at any function: nothing too controversial or profound, often caustic, but wide-ranging, and sometimes witty.

The vicar arrived next, minus his wife who had a chill and was unwilling to risk the snow and the cold, however picturesque the scenery by street-lamp. Mr Simon Thew was tall and thin, bald and stooped, a great lover of opera, an ornithologist of some local repute, something of a scholar. Patience was not perhaps his chief virtue, which might be considered by some a shortcoming in a man of the cloth, but he was a warm person, if a bit vague, and, since he lacked ambition, life at Halton Thoresby suited him admirably, as it had done these last twelve years. His wife was the daughter of his first rector, and they set a good example of marital harmony.

Last of all, as befits the local gentry, the occupants of the manor knocked on the door of Anchor Lodge and were readily admitted by Austin Vickers as his wife circulated the first of the canapés to those who had already arrived. Mr and Mrs George

Linford were not much loved in the village. They gave themselves airs to which, it was whispered, they aspired through money and not breeding. Mr Linford was an antiques dealer in Birmingham, where his premises occupied a swanky site in a well-to-do suburb. His wife Roberta was a school-teacher at a private boys' school in the neighborhood of Halton Thoresby. As in figure she inclined to flatness and in looks to plainness, even though she dressed with panache, the pupils made easy fun of her, but they respected her knowledge of her subject, which was French, and on the whole responded to her efforts to inculcate a knowledge of French culture and language in all-too-often recalcitrant youths. She taught Spanish as a side-line, if required.

A log fire in the grate shed a flickering light across the sitting-room, which was where most of the party usually assembled on these occasions, although sometimes they spilled into the hall or even the kitchen. Two elaborate standard-lamps provided extra illumination. Chairs were moved to the wall so that the guests could mingle freely. Mrs Vickers thought that if her guests sat, they would not mix, and to her way of thinking, a good evening was one spent with a variety of conversations–'no getting bogged down', she would say. Pictures hung on the walls; family photographs stood on the upright piano; a variety of ornaments occupied window-sills and niches and small shelves. A tall but narrow bookshelf stood in one corner, displaying volumes on history, politics, the countryside; classic novels; some poetry. Volumes of crossword puzzles, some current glossy magazines and library books were scattered on the tables. It was a large, comfortable room.

As the squire (in inverted commas) and his wife were ushered in, the predominant conversation had turned to next year's summer fête, which was always a source of difficulty and tension: too many chiefs and an insufficient number of Indians.

'My dear Deirdre,' Helen Simpson was saying, 'you cannot be serious about a bouncy castle.'

'We had one last year, and it made a lot of money!'

Sally interposed. 'Yes, but it just doesn't fit with the gentility of Halton Thoresby. We're not just out to make money: it's an exercise in social cohesion and the promotion of certain values. What do you think, Vicar?'

Mr Thew cleared his throat, aware of a delicate moment.

'Well,' he began uncertainly. 'I, er, I … I defer to the Committee on this point!'

The arrival of the Linfords saved him from further embarrassment. There was a general rearrangement of persons as the new arrivals were invited to shed their outer garments, took a glass of something warming and greeted the other guests already assembled.

As the evening wore on, pleasantries and topics of village life were exhausted, and conversation, by general agreement, took on a more serious tone. At one point Austin Vickers turned to Dismore and asked whether he were a religious man.

'No, not particularly. Brought up on it, of course, like so many people, but I've gradually faded away. Perhaps I shouldn't be saying this with the vicar at my elbow.'

'Don't worry about me,' said the Rev. Thew. 'You'd be amazed at the number of people who take pride in admitting how little religion means to them. Of course, that doesn't mean they're not spiritual, or that they don't believe in God, the afterlife or the soul.'

'I'm delighted you're so broad-minded, Vicar. I suppose I believed in God, the afterlife and the soul at one time, but I like to think I've graduated beyond them.'

'Come, come, Thornton,' said Matthewson, 'you don't mean that. How can an educated person not believe in the soul, for example?'

'OK, have a go at convincing me.'

'Oh, well, that's a little tricky. Let me see. You must be aware of being more than body. Your body is limited in space and time, tied to the spot, so to speak, but in your aspirations, in your dreams, if you like, you can wander through the stars. Or take an idea in your head. What is an idea? It occupies no space that we can tell, and yet its power! It can drive people to great heights, to despair, to atrocities. If your body is material–extended in space and time–where does your idea reside and take root? No, no, my friend, take it from me, you have an immaterial side, a spirit, a soul, perhaps you could even call it your mind, which is intangible, indestructible, or your very personality, that which makes you you and nobody else; your inner core. I also believe that your soul survives the death of the body. Don't you feel the basis of an immortality deep within you?'

'No, actually, I can't say I do. But what do other people think?'

The Rev. Thew opened his mouth to speak, but Dismore cut him short.

'No, not you, Vicar. You're biased!'

Julius Matthewson decided to demonstrate his powers as a thinking person.

'Plato believed in a soul, you know. So did Aristotle. All the great thinkers up to about the eighteenth century did so. It seemed the obvious way to explain human superiority over the brutes. An impartial examination of one's innermost consciousness reveals an intangibility which explains our nature as persons of discernment, aesthetic taste, appreciation of the higher things of life.'

'Wasn't it Wilde who said something like, "Those who see any difference between body and soul have neither"?' This was George Linford.

'I can't say that seems to mean very much,' said Mrs Matthewson. 'I certainly believe in the soul.' She turned to Martin Gee.

'You're quiet, Martin. What's going on inside that head of yours?'

'Thinking, you know. Let me put another, related, question, to our resident panel. If memory is part of what we mean by personality or soul, is there such a thing as a collective memory? I've been thinking about this recently, in connection with a ghost story I was told the other week.'

'What was that?' asked Mrs Linford. 'I simply love ghost stories!'

'I went up to York for a couple of days and decided to visit the Treasurer's House behind the Minster. As we finished our tour, the guide took us to the restaurant, and there she told us the following story. The authorities decided to lower the floor of the cellar to make better provision for the restaurant, and work had not gone very far when the workmen uncovered a square yard or so of Roman cobbles, about nine inches below the surface. A noise was heard, as of tramping feet, and before their astonished eyes, a small squad of Roman soldiers marched through the cellar. As the soldiers passed over the existing floor level, the workmen could see their legs down to just above their ankles. When the squad crossed the revealed stretch of cobbles, however, the workmen could see the Romans' sandals.' He paused.

'Yes?' said Mrs Linford impatiently. 'What then?'

'Oh, that was the end of the story, but it set me thinking. What if it was the reverse of what we normally consider happens in ghostly apparitions? Instead of the soldiers coming forward into our time, the workmen were taken back to Roman York–Eboracum–by some sort of collective memory. Not their personal memories, you understand, but a memory lodged deep in their minds over the intervening generations.'

'That's all very well,' chimed in Mrs Linford, rising grandly to the occasion, 'but how do you explain that all the workmen apparently had the same slumbering memory?'

'That's where my theory falls down, of course,' said Gee, 'but I'm working on it.'

'Actually, that's not such a bad theory,' said Dismore. 'Personal and physical characteristics are passed down through families for many generations. I once knew a Campbell who was the spitting image of a portrait of the worthy Colonel of Glencoe fame painted three hundred years before. And if we believe in progress, the more vicious family traits are gradually weeded out over the centuries, leaving only virtue! I can't solve the riddle posed by your little York story, but the general lines appeal to me. Has no one else felt the power of genetic inheritance?'

'Doesn't make any sense to me,' said Gee. 'You are what you make of yourself, not what your genes make you.'

'It seems to me,' said Mr Vickers, 'that Mr Dismore is veering dangerously towards the idea of a super-race–or perhaps super-family would be more accurate in his case.'

'Well, dear,' his wife chipped in, 'at least he believes in some sort of force working in the human race to produce improvement. Why he seems reluctant to call it "God" I'm not quite sure.'

'Actually, I think the idea of progress is vastly overrated. Our own age has been every bit as savage and mindless as any generation in the past.' This was the Rev. Thew. He warmed to his theme. 'Two world wars, sundry minor wars, famine and genocide, fascism and dictatorship, a flourishing of new diseases–'

'Exactly, Vicar,' interrupted Dismore, 'how can you believe that God persists into the twentieth century with all that going on? You've whipped the rug from under your own feet!'

At that moment, the conversation was interrupted, to the consternation of all, by the falling of a small piece of wood, as if on cue, on to the hearth-rug. Feet scattered. Austin Vickers leapt forward and seized the offending wood in his bare hands, returning it to the grate.

'Well done, sir,' exclaimed Dr Simpson.

'Nothing to it,' said Vickers. 'You know very well, Wartenby, that hot coals and burning wood take a few seconds or so to make an impact, particularly if there is sweat on your hands. I remember Arthur C. Clarke explaining that years ago, when he was researching fire-walking. Little beads of sweat apparently make a cushion between your skin and the source of heat.'

'Just like you to take the mystery out of extraordinary feats,' said his wife. 'On Christmas Eve, of all times!'

'Why do you say that, Mrs Vickers? What exactly is the mystery you discern in Christmas?' asked Dismore. Some standing by considered it ungentlemanly of him to bait his hostess in this way.

'It is the mystery of God's condescension,' interjected Mrs Simpson, before Mrs Vickers could reply. 'God stealing down to take up his abode in a dark world. Of course, in the Antipodes it's the height of summer, but that doesn't spoil the mystery for us. Come, come, Mr Dismore, I don't think you're half such an unbeliever as you try to make out. Is he, Deirdre?' as she turned to Mrs Matthewson.

'My dear, take no notice of Dismore. He's a notorious flier of kites.'

'Now,' announced Mrs Vickers in a loud voice, 'we've probably had enough standing around, so I suggest we sit down for a couple of quick charades. What do you all say?'

It was agreed to have a round of charades; and so the evening drew to a cosy close. It was soon time to repair to the church for carols. All Saints was a gracious example of an English country church. It stood impassively in an ancient graveyard, shielded from the worst of the north blast by great yew trees centuries in the making. The perimeter wall was green with lichen. The headstones lurched disconcertingly at odd angles. There was, however, a nobility and a dignity in the place which are the natural features of the best of English churches. This night, all was white. There was no wind. A few early footprints led up the path to the south door, and lights showed inside, betraying the activities of a warden or a late flower-arranger or perhaps the organist. The Vickers' party was almost late for the first carols.

The Christmas service took its time-honored course. Well-honed carol succeeded well-honed carol. Candles flickered, too feeble to dispel the shadows in the timber roof. Then the service proper began. Parishioners read the lessons from the lectern, the vicar preached a sermon from the pulpit–not a particularly good one this year, it must be said in the interests of veracity, but at least it was earnest. Holy Communion followed in due course, after prayers to the Almighty for the well-being of travelers, countries at war, suffering humanity at large–a long list of the needy and the oppressed–and the well-being of royalty too, naturally. The service closed with a loud rendition of *Oh come, all ye faithful*, and the organist capped that with a Bach voluntary which set the rafters ringing.

'Good night, Vicar, and happy Christmas!'

'Good night, Mrs Evershed.'

'Good night, Mrs Ravenscroft'.

The congregation, warm with a good conscience, drifted into the silent morning, melting away to a night-cap and their beds. The church and graveyard fell still, to awaken to a still dawn.

There was one exception, however, which unfortunately introduces a jarring note into our story. On Christmas morning, Mr Oglethorpe, a retired painter, set out to walk his dog. He lived on the edge of the village, in a small cottage that he shared with his wife, and, not being a churchgoer, he had no need to adapt his life to the requirements of church attendance. He had risen a little after dawn, made a cup of tea for himself and his missus, which they consumed in bed, and then ventured forth briefly before breakfast to satisfy the dog's needs. Enchanted by the world he found outside, he extended his usual stroll to encompass first the village green, then the head of the lane that led to the hamlet of Oswaldthorpe, and finally to the lane that led out of the village to Bolham. Here an unpleasant surprise awaited this early Christmas Day walker, for in a ditch the unmistakable feet of a human person reared up as if to arrest the progress of any passer-by. It was Mr Gee, and, *triste dictu*, he was dead–very dead if the stillness and stiffness of the corpse were any guide.

II

We should always have ready two rules:
that there is nothing good or evil save in the will;
and that we are not to lead events but to follow them.
Epictetus, How we should bear sickness, liber 3, caput 10

Nicholas Hotham was feeling rather pleased with himself. The sun was shining, he was looking forward to *Rigoletto* at the opera with his wife that evening, and he had just run to ground, in a second-hand bookshop which he had not visited for years, a copy of Matilda Geren's *Cyclops*, in a 1757 edition: leather-bound and in reasonable condition.

The Hothams lived in a small palazzo in the Via dei Polacchi, not far from the Piazza Venezia. The palazzo had not the grandeur of some Roman palazzi, nor their fame; and the family had rented out a few of the upper rooms to genteel lodgers to help pay the exorbitant costs of running an old Roman residence. The house fronted directly on to the street, access being generally through a wicket set in huge wooden doors that were kept closed and locked. Three storeys of rooms rose into the roof: brick tiles on the floors, wooden beams exposed, windows opening on to a small inner courtyard or giving a glimpse of the busy streets below. It was gracious enough, but perhaps a little shabby in parts. The truth is that Nicholas Hotham had money–not a fortune, but more than a competence–but no aristocratic background, whilst his wife Elisa had the latter–she was the youngest daughter of Count de' Gracchi–but no money. The two had met whilst both students attending a year's History of Art course at the Accademia Gentili in Florence. Your chronicler does not wish to give the impression that the Hothams' marriage was one merely of convenience. No, they had met and met again, their relationship had blossomed, they had fallen in love and eventually they had married. It was fortuitous that his money could save from complete ruin the palazzo left to his wife by a deceased grandmother, which her father could not afford to maintain, and that, to the delight of his family, he married into the aristocracy, albeit foreign and albeit at a modest level.

The Hothams lived well enough, despite the drain on their resources represented by a seventeenth-century building that always seemed to be requiring attention, at huge expense. Their three girls were all educated privately. They employed a cook and a maid-of-all-work. They entertained, and they traveled. Nicholas was aware, however, that their funds would never match his wife's aspirations, and prudence was the order of the day. His money was inherited, not earned. It is hoped that the reader will not dismiss him out of hand as a wastrel, simply because he did not work as other folks work, enduring a daily grind and longing for retirement. His Yorkshire estates had been accumulated over centuries by worthy ancestors, and he knew it was his privilege and burden to consolidate and maintain this patrimony. Twice a year he traveled to the United Kingdom to oversee his property: agricultural dwellings, land-holdings, shares in manors, a few town-houses, in some cases entire hamlets. He met his lessees, collected rents, inquired about damage, repairs and general maintenance, kept appointments with his accountant and his broker, kept abreast of building developments and the possibilities of compulsory purchase or bypasses or the construction of housing estates that might affect the value of his properties. He could, he supposed, employ a steward, but apart from saving the cost of a steward, he enjoyed his biannual visits to the land of his fathers and the work that he undertook there.

Nicholas and Elisa's daughters were the envy of their friends: charming girls, bred to captivate and enthral, clever, modest, pretty. Carolina, the eldest, was seventeen: a quiet person, given to solitary reading or thoughtful walks through the Roman streets and parks, but her large brown eyes had a fire and a depth that boded ill for hapless males who came within their purlieus. Renata, two years her junior, was musical, sports-loving and outgoing. Eufemia, finally, at twelve, was the darling of the household: a spoilt child, wayward, given to fits of ill-temper, but generally vivacious. All three girls were bilingual, this being a policy agreed on by the parents at the very outset. That is to say, Mrs Hotham senior insisted that her grandchildren spoke a proper language–none of this foreign stuff for her; and how were they going to read Shakespeare if English were not their first language?–while the Count de' Gracchi would not have any granddaughters of his ignorant of the language of Dante (and of Boccaccio if they had been boys and robuster; how he would have liked three grandsons!).

'Right, girls,' said Mr Hotham one morning, as soon as the family were assembled for the family breakfast, which tended to be a mixture of English and Italian custom. 'Where would you like to go for a holiday this year?'

'Ooh, I fancy South America, *babbo*. What about Patagonia? Just think of all those gorgeous cowboys, shining with good-health and good-humor!' said Renata.

'No, no, Rena,' said her elder sister, 'I should prefer somewhere less exotic, somewhere where we can soak up European culture. What about the Rhine Valley, Dad? We've never been there.'

'That's soppy,' retorted Renata, 'all churches and museums, I bet. We need to see the great open spaces of the world and a way of life we're not familiar with. We've been looking at South America with Signor Moltado in geography. It's fascinating.'

'I daresay, but the fact is that Germany will take you on an inner journey that's much more exciting and valuable than looking at a few cowboys running about vast open spaces.'

Mr Hotham interrupted.

'OK, you two, let Eufi have a say!'

Eufemia, however, was deep in a *fumetto* and deigned to speak only when thus addressed directly.

'I don't mind,' she said, 'as long as I can get away from Rena and Lina.'

'Now, dear,' said her mother, 'that's not the spirit. If we go on holiday, we all go together, and that's that.'

'In any case,' said Mr Hotham, 'a holiday for five to South America is likely to prove very expensive, and this year we need to repair the roof over the east side of the courtyard. So I agree with Lina, that we need somewhere closer to hand.'

And so the discussion continued. When the time for school came, the only agreement was that Mr Hotham would go to a travel agent and seek out a few brochures. He promised to do this that very morning.

He and the Count's daughter sauntered out into the Via dei Polacchi, she turning right for an appointment with her hair-dresser, he left towards the Piazza del Gesù in search of a travel agent. He pottered down the Via Celsa, into the Via del Gesù and so into the Via del Pie' di Marmo. It was at this point that he stopped remembering anything about that morning. A scooter came tearing round the corner, and the collision was painful for both concerned. Passers-by gathered up the unconscious Mr Hotham, and in no time at all he was safely in bed at the Ospedale of the Fatebene Fratelli, sedated against the pain of quite serious injuries.

Mrs Hotham was back at home, hair suavely coiffed, seated at the piano, trying to get her fingers round Henselt's *La Fontaine*. The difficulty, she found, was to apportion the arpeggios to best effect between the two hands.

'If it please *la Signoria Vostra*,' announced Maria the maid, 'there's a phone-call for you. They say it's urgent.'

'Urgent? For me? Surely not. But thank you, Maria. I shall take the call in the parlour.'

'Thank you, *Signora.*'

'*Pronto*! Mrs Hotham speaking.'

'Mrs Hotham, it's the Ospedale dei Fatebenefratelli. Your husband has been brought in after a small incident in the street, and we think you ought to be at his bedside.'

The long and the short of it was that Mr Hotham was conscious–just–but suffering from internal injuries for which an immediate operation was advised. The hospital authorities wished the couple to be informed that a serious operation always carried some risk, and it would be on their, the authorities', conscience if they proceeded in the circumstances without full consultation with the patient and his family. The operation was carried out, the process of recovery took its course, and finally Mr Hotham was returned home for the final stage of his convalescence.

It was one evening at this time that Mrs Hotham raised the question of her husband's will. The party was of the smallest: Mr and Mrs Hotham and two friends of theirs, Giulio and Liliana Sangallo, whom Mrs Hotham had met through the children's school. The conversation had turned to Voltaire's *Oedipe*, a rare performance of which had recently been presented at the Teatro Cimabue. Was it artistically legitimate to use an ancient myth as a vehicle for modern satire?

'Voltaire could always claim,' said Mrs Sangallo, 'that his intention had not been in any way satirical, that he simply wished to present Oedipus' dilemma to a contemporary audience.'

'In the event he made a bad calculation,' said her husband. 'In any case, it's a misuse of the myth to turn it into something it was never intended to be.'

'How do you know what it was intended to be?' asked Mr Hotham. 'Freud was right when he said that the Oedipus myth is timeless and multi-layered. You can apply it to all sorts of situations.'

'Quite apart from wanting a smokescreen behind which to conceal his satire,' said Elisa, 'the language is clumsy because the myth doesn't really lend itself to artificial criticism of a situation centuries removed. What about the lines

Our priests are not what foolish men have said:
Of our credulity is their whole science made?

They're a crude attempt to inject into the myth an element that just isn't there. Voltaire deserved his week in the Bastille for that alone!'

'Now you're being facetious, Elisa,' said her husband. 'No, I can see arguments on both sides, but the crucial question is why playwrights like Voltaire have to exploit an ancient subject in order to be critical of the authorities of their time. Why can't they just invent a new situation?'

'Oh,' said Mrs Sangallo, 'it's much more satisfactory to deal a covert blow with a theme the authorities themselves should be familiar with.'

'The play actually set me thinking in quite a different direction,' said Giulio. 'Here's a man, Oedipus, apparently totally successful in life, when all of a sudden his world collapses about him through absolutely no fault of his own. He is unprepared for any part of the catastrophe, and his response is a terrible gesture based on raw emotion rather than cool reason. His tragedy is not that he is the plaything of the gods–we are all that–but that his unconcern leaves him defenseless in the face of disaster. He has no inner resources with which to plan his response.'

There was a silence after the delivery of this little speech.

'OK,' said Mr Hotham, 'what should he have done after the truth of his situation had been revealed? How could he have prepared himself for what was after all a bolt from the blue?'

Giulio thought for a moment.

'I don't mean that he should have prepared himself for this particular blow, which as you say he could not have foreseen. He should have lived as if his life could and would collapse at any minute, so that he didn't sink with it but rose above the ruins. You can't predict every eventuality, and life would be miserable if you always expected the worst, but reasonable precautions can be taken: a spirit of detachment, order in one's affairs, a consciousness that one's dependents are cared for–that sort of thing.'

'I see,' said Nicholas. 'Interesting. I'd not seen things in quite that light before. Say that my accident had turned out for the worse. Where would Elisa and the girls be? Oh, dear, have I neglected my duties in life?'

'Have you made a will, for a start?' asked his anxious wife.

'Well, no, actually: wills are for old people to make, aren't they?'

As the American writer Austin O'Malley said, 'The man that leaves no will after his death had little will before his death'.

The conversation continued on to different topics, and the guests eventually left the Hothams to themselves.

It was some weeks later, as the Hothams elder were at lunch in the seclusion and privacy of their dining-room, that Nicholas held before him an open letter, with a furrow in his brow.

'My dear,' he began, 'I have received an extraordinary letter this morning, and I'm not quite sure what to make of it. I take it to be a hoax, but in which case it is in very questionable taste.'

'Who's it from, Nicholas?'

'Someone who signs himself John Goode. Have you ever heard the name?'

'No, not to my knowledge. What's on the envelope?'

'Oh, that's quite in order: Egr Sig Hotham Nicholas, Palazzo Gravina, via dei Polacchi, Roma. Posted from London.'

'So what's extraordinary about it?'

'I think you'd better read it for yourself, Elisa, and then you can tell me what you make of it.'

Elisa took the letter.

Dear Mr Hotham (she read),

I hope you will not resent my liberty in contacting you without previous introduction. You will not welcome what I have to say, but I beg you to believe that I have no animosity towards you personally. How could I, since I have no personal knowledge of you? The aim of this letter is simply to acquaint you with a rather unusual circumstance of which you are a beneficiary but which actually falls to me to enjoy. When you have read the attached document, you will appreciate more fully that your position is untenable. I regret having to be the bearer of such bad news, but I too have a family to protect and cherish. Further, I am sure that you and I can reach some accommodation, so that your future is not jeopardized entirely and that you can continue to live in something approaching the Roman style to which you have become accustomed. I propose to contact you again in a month's time to solicit your answer. Hoping that this arrangement meets with your approval, I have the honor to be your devoted servant.

PS I beg you to read the will with the utmost care. The codicils also have their importance.

'Signed *John Goode*, and as you say posted in London. What on earth can it be about?'

'Perhaps you'd better read the attached document, Elisa.'

She folded the letter over and found stapled to it the following screed. It was neatly typed on plain A4.

In the name of God Amen. This is the last Will and Testament of me Joan Goode of Clifton Street in the Parish of Saint Mary le Bone in the County of Middlesex Spinster made in manner following I Give and Devize all and singular my Manors and Freehold Messuages Farms Lands Tenements and all and every my parts and shares of and in all and singular the Manors Messuages Farms Lands Tenements Hereditaments and Real Estate whatever whereof I am seized in Fee simple or wherein I have or am entitled to any Estate of Inheritance situate lying and being in the several Towns Parishes Fields Precincts or Territories of Aike Kellythwaite Kellythorpe Sunderlandwick Emston Callerton Great Naseby Little Naseby Cockleham Thelp Laythorpe Aislaby Burroughton and every or any of them in the said County of York and in Galtby and Lambton in the County of the City of York or either of them or elsewhere in that part of Great Britain called England with their and every of their rights Members and Appurtenances and also all that my whole and undivided third part or share of and in the Rectory or Parsonage and Mansion Place of Sillingsby in the said County of York and of all Glebe Lands Tithes Portions of Tithes and other rights and Hereditaments to the said Rectory belonging and also of and in all and singular other those Messuages Lands Tenements and Hereditaments whatsoever with their Appurtenances in Sillingsby or elsewhere in the County of York which have been granted and devized and are held by virtue of two several Leases for [illegible] and the Archbishop of York and the Dean and Chapter of the Cathedral Church of Saint Peter at York subject to the Rents Covenants and Agreements under which the same are respectively held unto Mrs Susan Ball of Clifton Street aforesaid Spinster and her Assigns for and during the term of her natural Life and with such power of raising the Sum of one thousand and Fifty pounds which I am indebted to her as hereinafter mentioned and from and after the Decease of the said Susan Ball I Give and Devise all my said Freehold and Leasehold Estates and parts and shares of Estates and all my right and Interest therein with the Appurtenances unto the Reverend Richard Plaxton of Halifax in the said County of York and his Assigns for and during the Term of his natural Life and from and after the Decease of the Survivor of them the said Susan Ball and Richard Plaxton I Give and Devise all my said Freehold and Leasehold Estates whatsoever and all my right and Interest therein respectively unto William Hotham second son of James Hotham late of Higham in the County of Surry Esquire his Heirs and Assigns for ever in Case he shall then be living and shall have then attained or shall afterwards attain the Age of twenty one years and subject to the condition of taking the Name and bearing the Arms of Goode hereinafter contained which the Family have borne for more than two Centuries But in case the said William Hotham shall happen to die before he attains the Age of twenty one years or shall attain that age and happen to die in the life time of the said Susan Ball and Richard Plaxton or in the life time of the Survivor of them Then and in either of such Cases I Give and Devise all my said Freehold and Leasehold Estates whatsoevere with the Appurtenances unto Robert Hotham his Heirs and Assigns forever in Case he shall be then living and shall have then attained or shall afterwards attain the Age of twenty one years and subject to the Proviso or Condition aforementioned But in case the said Robert Hotham shall happen to die under the Age of twenty one years or shall attain that Age and shall happen to die in the life time of the said Susan Ball and Richard Plaxton or in the life time of the Survivor of them Then and in any of such Cases I Give and Devise all my said Freehold and Leasehold Estates whatsoever to their several uses upon the Trusts to and for the intents and purposes hereinafter mentioned (that is to say) to the use of my Godson Thomas Metcalfe third Son of the Reverend Thomas Metcalfe of [illegible] in the County of Sussex and the Heirs of his Body and for Default of such Issue to the use of the second and other Son and Sons of the said Thomas Metcalfe the Father the Elder Son for the time being severally successively and in remainder one after another as they shall be in Seniority of Age and Priority of Birth unto the Heirs of the Body and Bodies of such Sons lawfully Issuing the Elder of such Sons and the Heirs of his Body being always preferred and to take before the younger of such Heirs and the Heirs of his Body Issuing and for Default of such Issue the use of the first and other Daughter and Daughters of the said Thomas Metcalfe the Father severally successively and in remainder one after another as they shall be in Seniority of Age or Priority of Birth and the Heirs of the Body and Bodies of such Daughter and Daughters Issuing the Elder of such Daughter and the Heirs of her Body to be preferred and to take before the younger of such Daughters and the Heirs of her Body Issuing and in Default of such Issue to the use of the said Richard Plaxton his Heirs and Assigns for ever provided always and I do hereby Declare my Mind and Will to be that it shall and may be lawful to and for the said Susan Ball by any Deed or Writing under her hand and Seal attested by two or more Witnesses to Charge all or any of my said Freehold and Leasehold Estates with the Payment of the said Sum of one thousand and Fifty pounds due and owing from me to her as aforesaid together with legal Interest and for the better levying and raising the same Sum and Interest by the same or by any other Deed or Writing to devise all or any part of my said Freehold and Leasehold Estates for any term or number of years so that the same be made redeemable on payment of the said Sum of one thousand and Fifty pounds and Interest Provided also and I hereby expressly require the said William Hotham and Robert Hotham and their Heirs and Assigns when and so soon as they shall severally come into and be in the actual possession of my Freehold and Leasehold Estates under and by Virtue of this my Will to take upon himself and themselves in perpetuity the Surname of Goode only and to bear in perpetuity the Arms of Goode only and in Case either of them or their Heirs and Assigns severally or together shall neglect or refuse so to do for the space of three Calendar Months next after they shall respectively so come into Possession then and in such Case it is my Mind and Will that my said Freehold and Leasehold Estates shall go over and be enjoyed by such person and persons who can prove beyond reasonable

Doubt that they are members of the Family of Goode originally of Kellythwaite aforesaid whether they have known me or of me or not In case this provision remains unfulfilled for the space of three years after my decease I do Further Declare my Will that it shall and may be lawful to and for the said Susan Ball and Richard Plaxton or their several Assigns when in Possession of the said Estates by Indenture under her and his or their hand and Seal to Devise or Lease all or any part of my said Estates unto any person or persons for any term or number of years in Possession and not in Reversion for the best and most Improved yearly Rent and Rents that can be had or gotten for the same without taking any Fine or income in respect of such Lease or Leases for the Enjoyment in perpetuity of any member of the Family of Goode who shall prove his or her Entitlement under the terms of this my last Will and Testament And with regard to all the Rent and Arrears of Rent which shall be due to me at the time of my Decease and all my Personal Estate whatsoever I Give and Bequeath the same unto the said Susan Ball absolutely she paying thereout all my Just Debts and Funeral Expences and all such Legacies as I shall by any Codicil to this my Will Give and Bequeath and I constitute and appoint the said Susan Ball sole Executrix of this my Will and revoking all former and other Wills by me at any time heretofore made I publish and Declare this only to be my last Will and Testament In witness whereof I have to the two preceding Sheets set my hand and to this last Sheet set my hand and Seal the twenty ninth Day of July in the year of our Lord one thousand seven hundred and ninety three–Joan Goode. Witnesses: Thos Dunn William Lancaster No 17 Kings Street Bloomsbury Lincolus Dun John Hewitt.

Underneath, after a short gap, were, as their correspondent averred, several codicils:

1st Codicil to my Will this 28th Day of April 1794 To my Old Steward Will: Hall & his wife to each twenty Pounds for Mourning

also to John Hall their Son who I hope will succeed his Father as Steward to the Goode Estate the Sum of one hundred Pounds and ten pounds for Mourning to Elizabeth Freeman if living in this Family as House Maid or in any other Capacity at the time of my Death the Sum of twenty pounds and ten pounds for Mourning

to Mrs Eliz Wilson the Sum of one hundred pounds besides what may be due to her for wages if she is living with me at the time of my Death and ten pounds for Mourning–Joan Goode

2nd Codicil To my niece Dorothy Parker ~~the Sum of two hundred pounds with~~ I bequeath as many Fifty pounds as I have received from her since my Nephew's death. Joan Goode

3rd Codicil To John Myott whether living with me or having left me the Sum of Five hundred pounds for his exemplary good behavior and attencion to me while in my Service and if he is in my Service at the time of my Death 10 lbs for Mourning if he leaves it at that time then to have the ten pounds without going into Mourning with what wages are due to him. Joan Goode

4th Codicil I bequeath to Miss Francis Blair the Sum of ten pounds per annum ~~provided she dont~~ for her Life Provided she dont go to India. Joan Goode

5th Codicil I also Bequeath to my Faithful Servant John Myott if living with me at the time of my Death the yearly Sum of twenty pounds Per Annum for his natural Life Provided he neither sells nor Mortgages it the first payment of the said Annuity to commence one year after my Decease–Joan Goode

6th Codicil I appoint John Hall of Scorborough near Beverley the Steward of my Estate which I have in my own disposal–Joan Goode.

Scrawled in the margin were the words 'Not strictly relevant but interesting!' and the following paragraph ensued:

Appeared Personally Elizabeth Wilson of Hammersmith in the County of Middlesex Spinster and having duly sworn to depose the Truth made Oath that she knew and was well acquainted with Joan Goode formerly of Clifton Street in the Parish of Saint Mary le Bone in the County of Middlesex but late of Hammersmith in the same County Spinster Deceased for several years before and to the time of her Death which happened on or about the twenty Fifth Day of January last and that on the twenty sixth Day of the said Month of January last the last Will and Testament of the said Deceased hereunto annexed and also the paper writing likewise hereunto annexed beginning thus "1st Codicil to my Will this 28th Day of April 1794" ending thus "6 Codicil I appoint John Hall of Scorborough near Beverley the Steward to my Estate which I have in my own disposal" and thus subscribed "Joan Goode" were found by this Deponant in a Trunk or Box belonging to the said Deceased in the Parlour adjoining to the said Deceased's Bed Room and this Deponent Further made Oath that at the time the last mentioned paper writing was found as aforesaid she particularly observed that the words "the Sum of two hundred pounds" in the 2d Codicil written on the said paper were obliterated and that a Slip had been cut from the bottom of the said paper which Contained as this Deponent verily believes the third Codicil to the Will of the said Deceased and that having now with Care and attention viewed and perused the said paper writing she this Deponent says that she doth verily and in her Conscience believe that the said paper is now in the same Plight and Condition as it was at the time of the Death of the said Deceased and she does likewise believe from the Circumstances of the said Papers or Will and Codicils of the said Deceased being found as aforesaid that the said obliteration was made and the said slip Cut from the said Paper by the Deceased–Elizabeth: Wilson

'Nicholas, what on earth can all this mean? I am completely in the dark! If it's not a hoax, it's surely complete nonsense. What have we to do with anyone called Goode? And a will made two hundred years ago? I just don't understand at all.'

'I'm not quite sure myself,' said Nicholas.

He was in fact as puzzled as Elisa. If the arrival of the letter surprised him, however, it was only because he was unaware that anyone could be desiring to encompass the death of Mr Martin Gee.

Truth will come to light;
murder cannot be hid long.

William Shakespeare, The Merchant of Venice, Act II, Scene 2

As can be imagined, Mr Oglethorpe wasted no time in returning home and contacting the local constabulary. He thought it more politic, so early on Christmas morning, to phone than to call at the police-station in person.

'Constable Pudden,' he began, 'I have just found a body, and I know who it is.'

'Who is that speaking?'

'It's Oglethorpe, Constable. You know, the painter from Lace Lane.'

'Ah, yes, I know you. You say you've found a body. Is it dead?'

'Of course it's dead, Constable. It's Martin Gee: I recognized him from his gaiters.'

'Who's Martin Gee?'

'You know, that chappie in Rummer Row what writes books about art and what have you.'

'Oh, I know him. Why didn't you say so before? Where is he now?'

'He's upside down in a ditch in Bolham Road. If you meet me on the green in a few minutes, I'll take you there.'

'Right-ho. Give me time to get properly dressed. Must have my uniform on, you know.'

The constable had not had a cadaver to deal with in all his years at the village. When they arrived at the spot in question, it took him no time at all to concur with Oglethorpe's diagnosis.

'You know what it looks like to me?' said Oglethorpe, aspiring to impress the constable. 'He had too much to drink, fell into a ditch, and Bob's your uncle on a night like last night. No one could survive for long in a ditch. You couldn't, nor I couldn't, even if we was stone cold sober and not three sheets to the wind like this poor chappie evidently was.'

'Well, you may be right at that, but we'd probably best wait for a specialist opinion. Don't you go spreading it round the village that Gee couldn't hold his liquor!'

At that, he proposed that Oglethorpe wait by the body while he, Pudden, ran–or slid and slithered–home to phone the police station in Cannington to arrange for a pathologist, the usual photographic team and an undertaker–all, unfortunately, on Christmas morning. In due course, the body was removed, and inquiries began.

Constable Pudden's first port of call was Mr Gee's neighbors. Did they know at what time Mr Gee had left home? Oh, yes, they knew he had gone to the Vickerses' party–he always did–and on to church for the midnight service. That had been his intention, anyway. He had left home at about 8 o'clock. If he had gone to the service, he would have been on his way home at about a quarter to one. It was not quite a mile from the church to Rummer Row. This information prompted the constable to call at the vicarage, but there he got no reply, despite banging fairly heavily on the front door. Perhaps the vicar was already at the church for the eleven o'clock service; his wife might be having a lie-in and would be reluctant to appear in her negligé. He therefore went round to the Vickerses', and Austin Vickers answered his knock with a surprised look.

'Good morning, Constable. What on earth can have prompted you to call on Christmas morning? Nothing serious, I hope. Come on in.'

'I won't, thank you, Sir. I've come round to ask whether you know of Mr Gee's movements last night.'

'Mr Gee? Good heavens, nothing has happened, has it? Why, he was here with us until 11.30, and then we all went across to the church for carols and the midnight service. What's wrong?'

'Well, I suppose I can tell you,' said PC Pudden a little reluctantly, 'as it will soon be common knowledge. Mr Gee's body was found this morning on the Bolham Road, and I should say he had been dead some hours.'

'Goodness gracious, that is sad news. What on earth could have happened? He was perfectly all right when he left here. Anybody at the party can vouch for that. Is there anything I can do?'

'No, thank you, Sir. The Cannington police have removed the body, and appropriate procedures are in place. I'm just making a few preliminary inquiries while memories are fresh and the folks who might know something still about. You were at the midnight service, I take it, Sir. Can you tell me whether Mr Gee stayed to the end, and whether he went home alone or in company?'

'I'm sorry, I can't tell you anything. My wife and I sat near the front, and when we came out we, like everybody else, were anxious to get home on such an inclement night, and I took no notice of other people's movements. We had wished all our guests Happy Christmas at the house, and we therefore had no need to linger on after the service, except to give a quick greeting to one or two people we hadn't seen in the church. But some of the other worshippers might remember.'

'Thank you, Sir. Most helpful'–even though it wasn't. 'Can you give me the names of anybody else at the service who might remember something?'

'Well, most of the older people of the village were there. The younger couples, particularly if they have children, prefer to attend the Christmas morning service, as you know. Try Mrs Southby at the inn, or old Mr Thwaites at Green End–almost any of the older villagers, in fact. Sorry I can't be of more assistance.'

'One more thing, Sir, if you don't mind, and I'd appreciate it if you wouldn't mention this to anyone else at the moment. Had Mr Gee had a lot to drink at your party?'

'Oh, I don't think so. I've never seen Martin the worse for wear. Of course, I didn't keep a tally of what everyone was drinking, but I'd be very surprised to hear he'd had more than two or three glasses of wine–very.'

'Thank you, Sir. Might I come back a little later just to get off you the names of all your guests? You never know, one of them might have seen something or heard something.'

'Not at all, Constable. You will be most welcome.'

The constable's inquiries round the village eventually elicited the information he required. Mr Gee had accompanied the Vickerses' party to the church, had there sat towards the back, was one of the first to leave and was seen to head off towards the Bolham Road and home. He appeared perfectly ordinary: nothing to suggest unusual intoxication. Yawning, clearly tired, but then all the congregation were, at a quarter to one in the morning on a bitterly cold night. Constable Pudden could not ascertain who was the last person to see Martin Gee go off into the night, but then, although it had temporarily stopped snowing, everyone was anxious to get home, and why in any case should anyone take notice of who left the church when? Gee's footprint's in the snow had long since been covered by a fresh fall, and Mr Oglethorpe had no recollection of any footprints in the Bolham Road before his own. There were certainly none beyond the point where he had found the body; or vehicle tracks, if it comes to that.

None of this was very satisfactory, as it yielded no clue as to why Mr Gee should fall into a ditch on his way home *and stay there*. It wasn't a particularly steep ditch; there was no obvious object on which he could have concussed himself. If he was not intoxicated, why hadn't he simply scrambled to his feet and continued home? There was no sign at all that he had made any effort to save himself from falling–arms outstretched, for example–or set himself upright once he had fallen. He had been found with his head at the bottom of the ditch, his feet on the verge, and no suggestion that he had moved after falling. Heart attack, possibly? Stroke? It was all a bit of a puzzle.

The constable then went home to his lunch. After all, the discovery of a corpse was no reason that he could see to miss his turkey and trimmings. The only sop he made to 'procedure' was to phone Cannington to say that he would be continuing his inquiries shortly and that he would report back as soon as feasible. The autopsy, he learnt, would not be until the following day, and he replied that he would appreciate being informed of its findings.

After lunch–not too hurried a lunch–Constable Pudden set off on his rounds again to see whether he could find out more about Mr Gee's state at the conclusion of the party and in the church itself. A dratted nuisance on Christmas Day. He obtained the guest-list from Austin Vickers and determined to visit all the guests that very day if he could. Then he could justifiably put his feet up for the evening: perhaps a decent film on the telly to watch with his wife, or a spooky play on the radio.

He managed to see the Matthewsons, the Linfords and the Simpsons, without spectacular result. The Rev. Thew concurred with Mr Vickers' view that Martin Gee did not show any signs of excessive consumption of alcohol, either during the evening or at the service. Had he gone up to the front to receive Holy Communion? The vicar could not be sure, but he thought he had. No problems there. It was beginning to look as if Mr Oglethorpe's original mischievous diagnosis was mistaken, and that Mr Gee's death would have to be attributed to a medical cause such as heart failure. Sad, but these things happen. And the constable was not sure that Mr Gee would be much missed.

However, matters took on quite a different complexion on Boxing Day morning, when, towards midday, Constable Pudden received a telephone call from the Cannington police-station, informing him of the result of the post mortem. The pathologist, Dr Stanley Billings, had phoned for the station sergeant, but the latter was enjoying time off, and the doctor therefore perforce gave the gist of his report to the constable in charge.

'Well, there were no signs of violence to the body: no cuts, punctures, shot-wounds, bruises or anything of the kind. There was no degeneration or perturbation of the vital organs. He was not suffering from any pathological condition that I could determine: to all intents and purposes a completely healthy individual.' There was a pause.

'Yes, Doctor. I think I follow that. So what did he die of?'

'Hypothermia. No doubt about it. Classic symptoms: macular hemorrhage of the gastric mucosa, depletion of hepatic glycogen and so forth.' Another pause.

'Go on, Doctor. I sense you have more to say.'

'Well, your sergeant might like to know that Martin Gee had ingested a largish dose of digitalis. The effect of this could have been to make him so drowsy that he would wish to lie down–or in his case, seemingly, to fall down. He lay there sleeping in the ditch, and the cold killed him.'

'I see.'

'Tell your sergeant that death occurred at approximately half past one in the morning. Allowing for the action of the cold, the digitalis would have had to be ingested well before half eleven. Your sergeant will realize that anyone can produce digitalis from foxgloves, wild or domestic, if he knows what he's doing, except that the strength and composition of the result would be very difficult for an amateur to gauge. It is in theory possible that Gee made and took an infusion or tincture himself; you will have to consider this. But there are one or two odd points. Firstly, there was nothing on his person to indicate that he had been carrying the drug in any form on him: no phial, capsules, tablet-box, that sort of thing. Secondly, his heart was quite healthy, so why was he taking digitalis? Thirdly, even if he were, neither the time nor the place seems appropriate to the taking of medicine. Because of this suspicion of foul play, I believe the County have invited their CID to look into the matter. You will be hearing more in due course, I daresay. Well, good morning, Constable.' And Dr Billings was off the line. Here was a turn-up for the books! Murder in Halton Thoresby? Surely not!

That afternoon, Detective Inspector Wickfield and Detective Sergeant Spooner of the County CID arrived in the village to make initial inquiries into what had now become a possible murder investigation. The former was a large, florid man, balding, with bushy eyebrows and a great hooked nose. His lips were thin; his general demeanor purposeful but not without humor. His wife was receptionist to a medical practice in Bolham and mother of his two sons, neither of whom, having experienced for themselves, in their father's person, the hours worked by a policeman, had any intention of entering the police force. The inspector's sergeant on this occasion was an experienced detective in his early thirties, keen to do well and earn promotion. He was a married man, with an infant daughter on whom he doted. His wife served in a shop in Cannington. In appearance he was what in the olden days would have been called comely: good clean features, an intelligent eye, a pleasant manner, and always neatly turned out. Detective Inspector Wickfield had high hopes for his junior.

'I'll tell you why we're here, Spooner,' said Wickfield. 'A man doesn't take a hefty draught of a heart drug just before setting off for a midnight service, especially when he knows he's got a fifteen- or twenty-minute walk in the snow afterwards. Side-effects of a large dose can be socially embarrassing as well as dangerous, and I don't accept that Martin Gee would attempt to treat himself with digitalis without knowing something about what he was letting himself in for. No substance was found in his pockets when the body was removed. He could, of course, have swallowed tablets or a liquid preparation during the service, but we think that would be an unusual procedure. The suspicion is that he was fed the drug surreptitiously at the Vickerses' party, with the intention of making him drowsy or giving him a heart attack–the effects of digitalis being notoriously unpredictable–on his way home.'

'With respect, sir, have you checked whether Gee was in the habit of taking drugs for a heart condition?'

'No, we haven't had a chance yet, but it's on our agenda. That will be partly your job. If the drops, or less likely a tablet, were slipped into a glass of something at the party, the chances are that the person responsible had an eye to Gee's death in the snow. If Gee had been taken ill in the service, someone would have come quickly to his assistance, and remedies could have been applied. If, however, he had been taken ill after the service or at home, it would probably have been too late on a night like this. The murderer–let us call him so–would have anticipated that. He could not guarantee his victim's death, but he could have a good go. It is possible that, in his thoughts, if he failed this time, other opportunities would present themselves.'

'Could be a woman, sir.'

'So it could, Spooner. We shall keep our options open. As Saki said, women and elephants never forget an injury.'

'Could the drug have been in the communion wine?'

'Very doubtful. How do you lace a chalice so that only one person suffers? And how do you gain access to the chalice in the first place? No, no, we are looking at the members of the Vickerses' party as our pool of potential murderers. On the other hand–and it will pay us to keep an open mind–the deceased could have been dabbling in a little domestic preparation of digitalis. Say he was concerned about his heart but didn't like to trouble a doctor with the matter, or was frightened to in case it was bad news, and he decided to try a little herbal medicine on the side. No special equipment is needed in the case of digitalis, and the plant is common enough, heaven knows. The fact that it is a very difficult drug to manage effectively might not have occurred to him. On the other hand–again!–digitalis is a useful poison because it could point equally to accidental overdose or suicide as well as to murder.'

The situation looked a little implausible. Martin Gee was an aesthete and a scholar: a man of peace not of war, except perhaps a war of words. Constable Pudden had ascertained, which he guessed already, that Gee was not much *liked* in the village, because he was a little too precious for most people's tastes, but dislike was a long way from murder. Somewhere under the surface must lurk a hatred deep enough to move someone to take his life. The inspector realized that he needed a lot more information. He decided to start with a thorough search of Gee's cottage.

Rummer Row was a terrace of three houses on the Bolham road, originally, Wickfield surmised, farm-laborers' cottages. The two outer ones, of which one was Gee's, had been extended sideways to create reasonably spacious accommodation. Downstairs was a small hall-way leading to a kitchen on one side and a living-room on the other. On the first floor were two bedrooms and a bathroom, while the top storey contained a further bedroom and WC and an attic. The cottage was shiningly tidy. The search began downstairs, Wickfield taking the sitting-room, Spooner the kitchen. The sitting-room contained an ample library of works on art, some of them, of course, Gee's own books. Round the walls were mainly reproductions of Impressionist works. Three easy chairs, a television cabinet, a coffee table displaying art magazines, and a nice bow-fronted escritoire constituted the main furniture. On the mantelpiece stood a handsome bracket clock in an ebony case with metal mounts, by Charles Gretton of London. The bedrooms were sparely furnished: neat and elegant but lacking in warmth. The spare room bed was not made up, and the room contained nothing beyond the bed, two chairs and a dressing-table. A couple of Cézanne reproductions embellished the walls. Gee's own bedroom was plusher. A colorful quilt covered the bed: reds and soft browns with an elaborate pattern in gold. A wardrobe, a dressing-table, two Queen Anne walnut angle chairs, thick curtains, a deep carpet: the marks of a man of taste. None of these rooms held anything for the searchers, particularly not any signs of digitalis preparation. There were apparently no hidden cupboards or safe. All was above board, open to inspection.

The top floor yielded no secrets until the two men met in the attic. Here was the usual jumble of items that were not needed in the everyday but were too useful or valuable to be discarded: cardboard boxes containing who knew what, piles of papers, some books, a trunk or two, some odd bits of furniture, picture-frames, and so on. One item caught their attention in particular: a black metal box, locked in two places. A little violent persuasion encouraged the locks to part. There was little inside: family photos, some old school reports, a few papers like his birth certificate and degree diploma–and a newspaper cutting from the *Northumberland Times* of 1936. It was in an envelope of its own, but still discolored with age. Wickfield and Spooner read as follows:

Julius David Matthewson to Anne Rosemary Plumtre

On 13 October, the wedding took place between Julius Matthewson, 19, student, and Anne Plumtre, also 19, student, at St George's Church, Shoreland. The bride was given away by her father, Mr Gordon Plumtre, and was attended by Miss Seraphina Plumtre, her younger sister. The best man was Mr James Didcot. After a reception at the Three Falcons Hotel, the bride and groom left for their honeymoon abroad.

'Well, what do you make of that?' asked Wickfield. 'Why would someone keep a newspaper cutting locked away for over thirty years?'

'Perhaps he knew the people.'

'I think we need to investigate a little further. Wasn't Matthewson's wife called Deirdre on the list of guests Constable Pudden gave us?'

IV

Full little knowest thou that hast not tride,
What hell it is in suing long to bide:
To fawne, to crowche, to waite, to ride, to ronne,
To spend, to give, to want, to be undone:
Unhappie wight, borne to disastrous end,
That doth his life in so long tendance spend.

Edmund Spenser, Mother Hubbard's Tale, lines 895ff

Nicholas passed a sleepless night. He rose several times to re-read the letter and the will. At other times he made himself a drink, or took a short walk in the garden, or just lay in bed thinking. He even found himself praying for enlightenment. As the day dawned, he had come to a decision: he would go to England to speak directly with John Goode. It was intolerable that he should have to endure the suspense of not knowing precisely how the letter and will concerned him and Elisa, and what Goode's intentions were.

'Didn't you sleep, Nicholas? You were certainly very restless.'

'No, I couldn't sleep. Kept turning the problem over and over in my mind. But I've decided to go to England as soon as I can, today if possible, to see this man and find out what he's up to. I can't help feeling threatened, and I don't like it.'

'Are you any clearer on what it could all mean?'

'Yes, I think so,' said Nicholas slowly. 'A little. I've had time to re-read the will carefully and to come to grips with the impossible legal jargon these lawyer fellows insist on using. I kept thinking of Martial's epigram that lawyers "hire out their words".'

'So, what's it about?'

'This is how I see it, although I may be quite wrong. Joan Goode died in 1795 or thereabouts, a wealthy spinster. She was determined to leave her considerable estate to members of her own family who would carry the name and arms on into the foreseeable future–or really for ever. Unfortunately, she knew of none. Her immediate male family were all deceased, and, as she had moved away from Yorkshire, she was out of touch with other branches of the Goodes. She fixed on a family called Hotham–I've no clue why: perhaps he was a distant relation–and left everything to one of them, a young man William, on one condition: that within three months of coming into the estate, he should formally adopt the name and arms of Goode. So much for the will. Now we come to Master John's obnoxious letter. From this I gather that William Hotham did not abide by the terms of the will, either not at all or not fully, and that he therefore, in the understanding of Master Goode, forfeited the Goode estates.

'Now, here is something rather curious. Our own estate comprises land and properties situated in all the places named in Joan Goode's will, although I think some of the place-names have changed over the years. I therefore deduce that, according to John Goode, we have somehow come into possession of the Goodes' Yorkshire estate; and that further, because we don't bear the name Goode, whereas he does, we have no right to the lands and he has! He hints at "an accommodation". This is presumably a deal whereby he takes half, or three-quarters, or even perhaps all, of whatever we own in Yorkshire, in return for leaving us in peace. And that would be intolerable. But I'm only guessing what he could have in mind.

'So I have determined to see this bounder and find out exactly what he wants with us. It could all be bluff, or an elaborate hoax, but I need to find out. Do you agree?'

'Certainly I do, *amore*. Do you want me to go with you?'

'No, that would mean making arrangements for the children, and I'm not sure that two of us would do any better than one. We'll put our heads together when I get back.'

There was no telephone number on John Goode's letter, and a call to a directory produced no result. Nicholas had therefore no choice but to fly to London and hope that his quarry was in residence. Flying out of Fiumicino later that afternoon, he wondered whether he was on a wild-goose-chase. If he was not, how serious was the threat to himself and his family? What might the consequences be of Goode's impertinence and machinations?

A bus into central London and a taxi thence brought him to the door of Flat 33, Graham Mansions, Gilmore Road, Tooting. It was not a prepossessing neighborhood; it was not a prepossessing block. The stairwell was decayed and malodorous, and Nicholas' heart misgave him as he trudged up the scruffy stairs. At length he knocked at the door of No.33, nervous and uncertain. There was a pause, a noise of shuffling, and the door opened to reveal a man of about his own age, in carpet slippers and holding a newspaper.

'Yes?' was the opening syllable.

'My name is Hotham, Nicholas Hotham. You wrote to me in Rome.'

'Mr Hotham! This is an unexpected surprise, and indeed a great pleasure. I had not expected to meet you so soon. But come in, come in. You are indeed welcome.'

The flat was clean and reasonably well furnished. An entrance hall-way led to a kitchen on the right, a bedroom on the left, a little passageway going presumably to a bathroom and perhaps another bedroom, and a comfortable living-room. Nicholas noticed that the bed in the first bedroom was double. There were a few feminine touches in the flat: a sewing-box, a bowl of flowers, a lady's scarf on the back of the sofa, but the lady of the house was clearly not in at the moment. A large bookshelf in the living-room betokened an education and the interests of a reading man: international finance, novels in French, books on World War II. One section of the bookshelf was devoted to genealogy: dictionaries of surnames, box-files labeled 'Parish Registers', 'Birth Certificates', 'Pedigrees', 'Census Returns' and the like, dictionaries of place-names, local histories, stacks of papers. His heart sank: perhaps Goode did know what he was talking about after all. There was, however, no need to get despondent before the interview had even begun!

Goode offered him a drink: a G & T? tea? Had he eaten? No, he had not eaten, but he would like to discuss the matter in hand without more ado. A dry sherry, though, would be welcome.

'Now then, Mr Goode, perhaps you could explain to me what this is all about. I've traveled a considerable distance, and I should appreciate plain speaking. I am presuming this is not a joke.'

Nicholas had taken an immediate dislike to the unctuous Mr Goode.

'No, no, dearie me, certainly not a joke. I am quite in earnest. I hope you and I can come to an amicable arrangement, however, and that there is no need for unpleasantness.'

'Please begin.'

'Very well. I think it probably best if I go right back to the beginning, if you will bear with me, but let me say first of all that I can prove all I am about to say: I have in my possession all the relevant documents, or at least perhaps I should say copies of the relevant documents, and that there can be no mistake. I am right. I began the study of genealogy many years ago, and I know what I am about. It has taken me many years to amass the information I am going to lay before you and to substantiate it to my satisfaction.

'Our story begins in about 1500. In that year, roughly, two brothers called Goode crossed the Pennines from west to east and settled in Yorkshire. I believe, although I cannot prove it, that they were involved in the wool trade. They settled in villages a few miles apart. One brother, Adam, had the good fortune, or the wit, to marry an heiress, the daughter of Lord Mitcham, while the other, James, married more modestly and passes out of our story. Adam's marriage enabled him not only to lease a manor-house in which to reside in style, but also to purchase lands– the beginnings of the Goode estates. By the way, at that time, and indeed until considerably later, the family spelt its name as Goode, Goude, Goudde or Good, as the fancy took them, or as the clerks' fancy took them, but there can be no doubt that it is the same family throughout.

'Now Adam, who died in 1538, had two sons, James and Thomas, who in 1561 applied for and obtained a coat of arms, although I have my suspicions that they were using it before– legally but unofficially. It is significant that they offered no impressive pedigree to claim descent from a famous or a wealthy personage: they couldn't!

'I hope I am not boring you with all this?

'Anyhow, Adam's family prospered. In due course, as they purchased further lands and interests, they were able to buy a substantial property in Hull, to keep servants and to hobnob with the gentry. Their sons went to university; their daughters married sons of gentry. One of them became MP for Hull, and so on.

'However, things began to go wrong, in the sense that the male line gradually dwindled, until only one male was left, Colonel James, and he had no surviving sons, only daughters. It looked as if the family would die out as Goode, after nearly three hundred years of success. The final Goode was a spinster, Joan, who had moved to London, and in her will she took steps to ensure the continuance of the name, arms and estates. In this laudable intention she was thwarted, because the unworthy relative–pardon my plainness of speech, Mr Hotham–a certain Robert Hotham, to whom she bequeathed her property, did not carry out her explicit wishes with regard to the name and arms.

'Meanwhile, a younger branch of the family, descended from Adam's youngest son John, continued to prosper but in humbler fashion, not greatly distinguishing themselves in any field that I can discover. They became small farmers, weavers, carpenters and married their own kind. I can give you complete, documented and reliable trees of both families.'

He paused expectantly, and if he expected his listener to interject a comment, he was not disappointed.

'I see,' said Hotham. 'If I understand you correctly, I am descended from Robert Hotham and you from John Goode. What then?'

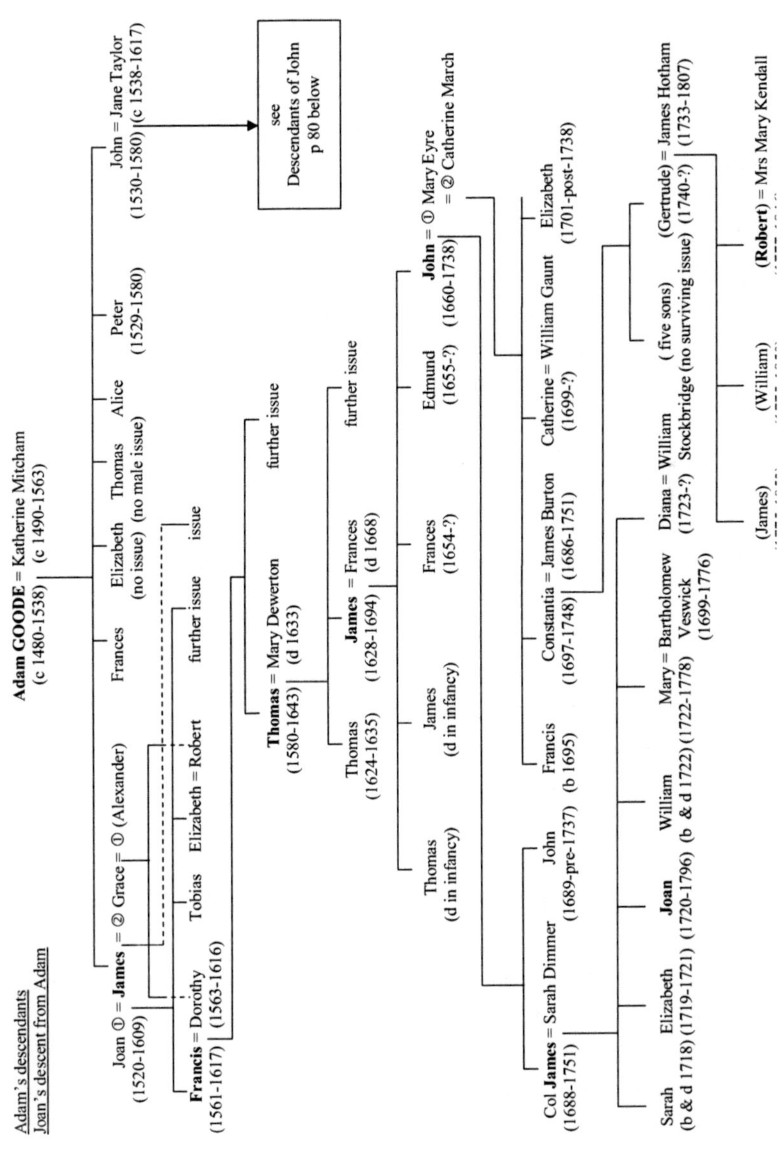
Adam's descendants
Joan's descent from Adam
Adam GOODE = Katherine Mitcham
(c 1480-1538) (c 1490-1563)
Joan ① = James = ② Grace = ① (Alexander)
(1520-1609)
Frances
Elizabeth
(no issue)
Thomas
(no male issue)
Alice
Peter
(1529-1580)
John = Jane Taylor
(1530-1580) (c 1538-1617)
see
Descendants of John
p 80 below
Francis = Dorothy
(1561-1617) (1563-1616)
Tobias
Elizabeth = Robert
further issue
issue
Thomas = Mary Dewerton
(1580-1643) (d 1633)
further issue
Thomas
(1624-1635)
James = Frances
(1628-1694) (d 1668)
further issue
Thomas
(d in infancy)
James
(d in infancy)
Frances
(1654-?)
Edmund
(1655-?)
John = ① Mary Eyre
(1660-1738)
= ② Catherine March
Col James = Sarah Dimmer
(1688-1751)
John
(1689-pre-1737)
Francis
(b 1695)
Constantia = James Burton
(1697-1748) (1686-1751)
Catherine = William Gaunt
(1699-?)
Elizabeth
(1701-post-1738)
Sarah
(b & d 1718)
Elizabeth
(1719-1721)
Joan
(1720-1796)
William
(b & d 1722)
Mary = Bartholomew
(1722-1778) Veswick
(1699-1776)
Diana = William
(1723-?) Stockbridge
(five sons)
(no surviving issue)
(Gertrude) = James Hotham
(1740-?) (1733-1807)
(James)
(William)
(Robert) = Mrs Mary Kendall

'Well, don't you see, your ancestor's actions have wiped out your title to any of the Goode lands, whereas Joan's explicit provision in the will means that I can stake a valid claim to the name–although that's already mine through right of lineal descent–and to the arms *and the estates*!'

There was a long pause while Nicholas tried to digest this information, watched carefully by his adversary.

'What if I simply laugh at your pretensions?'

'Well, you would be ill-advised to do so. I have spent years preparing my case, and I am now ready to do battle if it should come to that. I prefer to think that you will see reason and that we can reach a more or less painless agreement.'

'What do you want?'

'This is what I propose. You cede to me three-quarters of your Yorkshire estates and the right to bear the Goode arms, and I disappear from your life.'

'What if I refuse?'

'If you refuse, I shall resort to the law, challenging your right to the Goode lands. If the court finds in your favor, I shall come away with nothing but the ruin of my expectations. If, on the other hand, you lose–if, that is, the court finds in my favor–you could see yourself deprived of the entire estate and perhaps also obliged to pay me restitution amounting to many thousands of pounds. You would probably be beggared. Have to take your children out of private school. Give up foreign travel. You might even have to sell your Roman property. Not a pretty prospect, is it?'

'You're a fiend. What right have you to deprive me of all I hold dear?'

''What right have you to benefit from the fraud of an ancestor? My title to the lands lies in a valid will drawn up by a lady of means who had the family's interests deeply at heart. If right matters, you will wish to see her wishes carried out. If you can deny me and still live with your conscience after this conversation, I pity you.'

'Kindly show me the family trees.'

'Yes, of course. I have even prepared copies for you, and a copy of the arms, so that you can discuss matters with your lady wife in an informed way.'

'These can't be complete trees!'

'No, you're right. The complete trees stretch over many pages. All I have included here is the essential information in a handy form. You are welcome to see the complete papers, but I assure you that they add nothing further of substantial importance to what you have there.'

As Nicholas took a first look at the trees, Goode was expressing his deep regret that his wife and son were out for the evening and so would not be able to meet Mr Hotham on this occasion. Mr Hotham, however, with one eye on the documents in front of him and the other on his host, was beginning to doubt whether John Goode had a wife at all, much less a son. He seemed too intense and concentrated to be a married man. After a little more discussion, John Goode said:

'Well, Mr Hotham, so far so good: no fisticuffs as yet! I am sure we shall get on splendidly in the next stage of our talks. Shall we say that I shall expect to hear from you within one month from today? How does that suit?'

Thus ended this momentous and seismic interview. Nicholas saw his world crashing down about his ears. What a bolt from the blue! The destruction of life as he knew it. How could he face Elisa and the girls? Yet he must.

When he returned to Palazzo Gravina the following day, tired, confused and depressed, his wife naturally desired to know instantly what had passed at the interview. They sat together in the drawing-room, sad and apprehensive creatures at an uncertain cross-roads. A pot of tea lay on the beech-wood coffee-table, with a plate of biscuits and several home-baked muffins. The girls were ensconced upstairs, they presumed, in front of the television.

Nicholas gave as complete an account of his journey and meeting with Goode as possible. It was a narrative which, had they not been so intimately involved, might have been interesting.

'What are your thoughts so far, dear?' asked Elisa gently.

'That Goode is a swine and a devil and somebody should rid the world of him.'

'Yes, but apart from that? What are we going to do?'

'I don't know. If we go to court, the judge may find against us and we lose everything. Of course, he may decide that Goode has manufactured the evidence, that the law is not, after all this time, on his side, that he has no more right to the estate than we have–but the difficulty is, we just can't be sure. This is such an unusual case, I can't believe the judge will be able simply to apply a legal precedent. He may find against us but share the estate between Goode and us. On the other hand, he may decide in our favor, and then our nightmare will be over for ever–for Goode, as you might say. If he decides in our favor, he may still require us to take the sole surname of Goode and to demonstrate in some way our use of the Goode arms, but I think we can cope with that. However, whatever verdict the court reaches, there could be an appeal, and the case could drag on for years.'

'Is a court-case not a bit of a gamble for Goode as well?'

'Yes, it is. All his work and his aspirations could collapse, and he would presumably have to foot a legal bill to pay for being so vexatious, which won't be small, believe you me, but then he has very much to gain if he wins. On the other hand, he might prefer to keep a bird in the hand–the 75% share in the estate which he asked for–than to lose a bird in the bush. I have asked myself whether he would settle for 50% of the estate, which we could probably manage on by rearranging our life-style, but he's such a cold fish, so oily and sanctimonious, and so intense, that I doubt it. We could try–

'Oh, Nicholas, *amore*, this is quite frightful. How did you come into the estate in the first place? Had you any inkling that perhaps not all was well?'

'Not at all. I inherited the estate as a package from my father, he from his, and so on. All my linear male ancestors were eldest sons and heirs, and there has never been any suggestion in the family that our inheritance was improper or ill-gotten. No one has ever questioned our right to the properties, as far as I know.

I am prepared to believe Goode's account, since he seemed so well informed, with all the facts at his finger-tips as if he'd lived with them for years, and I'd be happy for the court to probe it. I doubt whether we've still got the necessary papers, which would presumably have to stretch back two centuries at least. In any case, it would, I imagine, be very expensive to commission an inquiry. We could look up wills, of course, but they won't tell us whether any of the titles was bogus or unjustified.'

The two were silent for a while.

'Should we tell the children?' asked Elisa.

'I think we must. They're old enough to grasp the essential situation, and we have nothing to gain from concealing a major trauma as this is likely to be. They are sufficiently resilient and intelligent not to fall apart; but I wish we didn't have to.'

'Goode's given us a month in which to make up our minds. What are we going to say?'

'I'll be guided by you, my dear. My own view is that we should fight it and let him take the matter to court if he so desires. And a pox on all his tackle. But should we try to negotiate first? It would be better to lose half the estate than all of it.'

'I'm sorry, my head is in a whirl, and I really don't know what course of action to take. Can we talk about it again in the morning? I may feel stronger. Have we any legal friends who could advise us?'

V

Thy hand, great Anarch, lets the curtain fall,
And universal darkness buries all.

Alexander Pope, The Dunciad, Book 4, lines 655-656

'Righty-ho, my lad, let's get cracking.'

Inspector Wickfield, his large face suffused with purpose and energy, his great nose pointing the way forward, launched what was to become one of his most confusing and intractable cases.

'You tackle the Vickerses and the Simpsons, I'll take the Matthewsons and the Linfords. We'll leave the Vicar until last, as I can't believe he's got anything to do with it. A man of the cloth? A septuagenarian living tucked away in a quiet rural vicarage? No, I don't think so, but we shall see. And remember, the murderer could have acted without the knowledge of his or her spouse. See you back at the station.'

Spooner called first on the Vickerses, the hosts of the party at which the victim had, it was thought, been fed the fatal drug–or rather, the drug that seemed to have proved fatal.

'Come in, Sergeant. Unpleasant job, yours, scratching around for evidence of skulduggery in such a peaceful and respectable community as ours. Myself, I think you're barking up the wrong tree, but you know your business best, I daresay. Old Gee took the pills himself, felt drowsy unexpectedly, and there you are.'

'Well, Sir, you may be right, but I'd just like to go through a few details with you.'

'Yes, of course.'

'Your wife at home, Sir?'

'No, she's doing a spot of shopping in Cannington. Can't see her being back for a while.'

'That's fine. I can catch up with her later. So, Mr Vickers, you've already told Constable Pudden,' he began, consulting his notebook, 'that you would be surprised if Mr Gee had consumed more than three glasses of wine during the evening. Could he have been drinking beforehand?'

'Nothing to stop him, I suppose, but look here, Sergeant, Gee was much too prim and proper to over-indulge. It would have been a disgrace to be seen in public even merry, let alone tipsy. Three small measures of wine over a whole evening, with food, would not be excessive, but I should be very surprised to see him exceed that.'

'How well did you know the deceased, Mr Vickers?'

'Quite well. He came regularly to the house–two or three times a year–and we met at the village fête, that sort of thing. Not a close friend, but more than a casual acquaintance.'

'I see. When did he take his last drink with you on the evening in question, do you know?'

'Sorry, no idea. The end of the evening rather caught us unawares, and we all hurried off to church, without taking much notice of who was where, with whom, doing what, you understand.'

'I see. Do you know of any enemies Mr Gee might have had, in the village or in his private life?'

Vickers said, 'Sergeant, this is Halton Thoresby, not Chicago. Nothing ever happens to ruffle the placid pattern of life here. You've only got to walk across the green to experience the extraordinary serenity of this corner of the English rural scene. The greatest upheaval in this village since old Farmer Scotney urinated in the pond in front of the lady of the manor in 1860-something was a spat between Gee and Linford six months ago, and it is quite certain that that has nothing to do with our present business. So no, I can't help you on that one.'

'Tell me about this "spat" anyway, if you please.'

'But it can't have any bearing at all. It was nothing–just a bit of local unpleasantness.'

'Perhaps if you tell me, Mr Vickers, I can judge for myself.'

'Oh, very well. It was like this. George Linford wanted some advice about a painting he was considering purchasing for their revamped drawing-room. He went to Gee. The picture was a Maupuis, I seem to remember, being offered at auction with a guide price of £3000. That's a lot of money, but the Linfords wanted a proper focus for the room that would impress their friends with their knowledge of modern art. I've added that last bit in, Sergeant. Naughty of me, really. Anyway, Gee went to inspect the painting, gave it the thumbs-up and added that, in years to come, its value would double and treble as Maupuis was gaining in popularity. George duly went to the auction, made the highest bid with that nonchalant wave of his, and what with commission and so forth, he forked out nearer £5000 than £3000. I was there at the time. Anyway, he took it home and gave it pride of place above the mantelpiece. It was a matter of weeks afterwards that the newspapers ran a story about fake Maupuis. The Linfords summoned an expert, and their painting was a forgery–not even a very clever one, said the expert. Not only had the Linfords lost quite a lot of money, they had been made to appear foolish in front of their friends and acquaintances, and that was something George couldn't forgive Gee. I remember his uttering blood-curdling imprecations, damning Gee as an amateur, a dilettante, a fop, a charlatan–etc!

'Having said all that, Sergeant, I must say that it's difficult to see George resorting to *murder* to get his own back. No, no, but you did ask me. That's the only incident of hostility I can think of.'

'Thank you, Mr Vickers, you have been most helpful.'

Next on his list were the Simpsons. Dr and Mrs Simpson occupied an imposing detached villa on the Cannington Road, on the edge of the village green. Double-fronted, sitting in its own garden, it exuded an air of well-to-do burgherhood. The doctor and his wife were just concluding a midday meal, and the former, in his own words, was about to take 'forty winks' to prepare himself for his afternoon visits, which would be followed by surgery at five. Wartenby wore old-fashioned side-whiskers.

He was in a tweed suit, the picture of an efficient professional man. His wife wore a plain two-piece. As she explained, she would shortly be attending a meeting of the WI, and she never liked to dress down for these occasions. The room into which the sergeant was ushered was a model of propriety, and the piano, and books on music, modern literary criticism and poetry scattered on tables imparted an erudite if somewhat earnest atmosphere.

The doctor was not encouraging.

'Look here, Sergeant, I appreciate that you have to make inquiries, but really, my wife and I are busy people, and I don't see how we can help you at all. We saw nothing untoward at the party, Gee seemed perfectly all right to me both there and in the church, and we've no other information to offer. Have we, dear?'

'But you did see Mr Gee in the church?'

'Yes, fleetingly, as he went up to receive communion. It all seemed perfectly normal to me.'

'What about you, Mrs Simpson?'

'Oh, yes, I agree entirely with my husband, Sergeant. I didn't notice Mr Gee in church, but at the party he was entirely himself, I should say, in so far as one can judge.'

'How well did you know the deceased?' This question was addressed to both indifferently.

The doctor jumped in quickly–a little too quickly, thought the Sergeant.

'Not very well at all. The Vickerses' soirée was about the only occasion in the year on which we met.'

'Did he have any enemies that you know of?'

'Well, I never particularly took to the man myself, and I'm not sure he was very popular in the village, with that mincing walk of his and his dandified airs, but I don't know of any particular hostility on the part of an individual who would wish to murder him.'

'When you say that you never took to the man, do you have a particular reason for saying that?'

Wartenby hesitated.

'Look here, Sergeant, we might as well tell you now, as you'll probably find out anyway, that Gee and I were engaged in a rather unpleasant dispute. He reported me to the General Medical Council for "deficient performance". Absolute nonsense, of course, I needn't tell you, but he initiated an investigation which has considerably unsettled me. It had to do with a course of antibiotics I prescribed which had unfortunate side-effects, and Gee blamed me for the deterioration in his condition. I can't say I'm sorry he's out of the way, as the action will now lapse in the absence of any accusatory testimony.'

'You would, of course, have easy access to digoxin, and you would know the exact dose to give.'

'Sergeant, I take grave exception to those remarks. I am as innocent of Gee's death as you are, and in any case, you have no right to scatter accusations in that offhand fashion. I think perhaps you'd better go if you don't wish me to take the matter up with your superiors.'

Meanwhile, the Detective Inspector decided to pay a visit first to the Matthewsons'. He was intrigued by the newspaper cutting found in Martin Gee's black box. He was not convinced that it had anything to do with the case, but one never knew. He turned over Dryden's couplet in his mind:

'He trudg'd along unknowing what he sought,
And whistled as he went, for want of thought.'

It was certainly true that he had precious little to go on, and he knew that there was little advantage in speculating in the absence of facts.

He decided to park outside the church and to repair to the Matthewsons' residence, which was only a matter of a hundred yards away, on foot, in the vague hope of receiving inspiration from the atmosphere of the village. It was cold but sunny. The snow lingered, but there had been no fresh falls for two days. The village lay tranquil in the dip of the hills. An occasional dog barked, and he could hear pigeons in the distance, but there was little other sound. The house he sought was a prosperous villa set back from the green and overshadowed by a great chestnut that seemed to jostle the house, solid though it was, into insignificance. He saw that the shrubs in the front garden were overblown: could the Mattewsons not afford a gardener, or did they not care that much? He knocked firmly at the front-door, noticing that the knocker, which seemed to him to speak of Mediterranean landscapes, depicted an olive-tree in silhouette; perhaps brought home from some foreign holiday. The man of the house himself opened the door.

'Detective Inspector Wickfield, Sir. I wonder whether I might have a word? It's about Mr Gee's death two days ago.'

'Yes, Inspector, I was expecting a visit before long: the whole village is buzzing with news of the descent of the CID. Come on in.'

He stood back to allow the inspector to walk into the living-room.

'Can I get you some refreshment?'

'Well, yes, actually, a cup of tea would be very welcome.'

While his host disappeared into the kitchen (he presumed), the inspector took the opportunity to glance over the spines of the books on the bookshelves. He was himself a keen reader, and he often thought that a man's bookshelf was as sure a guide to his inner self as anything. Novels, mainly Victorian English, but also Manzoni, Leopardi, a volume of Pirandello, a Dumas paperback; some more serious stuff–law-books (perhaps his main legal library was at the office), biblical volumes, philosophy (Wickfield remarked on Nietzsche and some heavier stuff: Hegel and Schopenhauer); and some travel books; the usual encyclopaedias and reference books.

'Well, now, Inspector, how can I help?'

'Did you know Martin Gee well?'

'Well, not well, exactly. My wife and I have been to his house a couple of times, and he has been round here to make up a bridge four, but we weren't close. I found him a curious character. On the one hand, he was cultivated and a good talker, but on the other, his camp mannerisms got on my nerves. But perhaps I shouldn't speak ill of the dead! Does that answer your question, Inspector?'

'Yes, thank you. Did you notice anything unusual at the party? Excessive drinking on Gee's part, for example?'

'No, not at all. He had always struck me as a moderate drinker, on the occasions when I have been in company with him. Why do you ask?'

Ignoring the question, Wickfield proceeded to the more delicate part of his inquiry.

'Mr Matthewson, there's something on my mind which I think you may be able to clarify for me. We found in Mr Gee's attic a newspaper cutting from thirty-five years ago in which your bride is named as Anne Plumtre. Can you explain this?'

'Yes, easily. Anne was my first wife. It didn't work out–perhaps we were both too young–and we eventually went our separate ways.'

'Can you imagine any reason Martin Gee might have for keeping that cutting? Was it of personal interest to him in some way, do you think?'

'I've no idea, I'm afraid, Inspector. Is there anything else I can help you with?'

'Mr Matthewson, I'm afraid you're not being quite honest with me, and I must have straight answers. I put it to you that there was something, shall we say dubious, about this marriage, and that Martin Gee was threatening you with his knowledge. Am I right?'

Julius Matthewson blenched and fidgeted. He was clearly suffering some great internal struggle.

'Inspector, can I ask you to preserve what I am about to tell you as deadly secret, particularly from my wife? The knowledge of it would devastate her.'

'Mr Matthewson, you know that in a murder inquiry I cannot promise to conceal from the authorities any information which I may consider relevant to the crime, but I give you my word that I shall not speak unduly of anything you may choose to tell me.'

'Inspector, this is very difficult for me. To put matters in their directest form, my present marriage is bigamous. Anne refused, and refuses, to give me a divorce because she is a Catholic. She believes that we are still married in the sight of God and that one day, who knows, we may get together again. I cannot convince her of the contrary. Needless to say, Deirdre knows nothing of this. As the cutting probably makes plain, that first marriage took place a long time ago a long way from here, and I hoped that it would never catch up with me.'

'Thank you for being so frank, Mr Matthewson. I believe you have told me nothing but the truth. Bigamy is a felony, punishable by law, but we may let it rest for the present; in any case there is not always a prosecution. Perhaps you should take steps to regularize your situation. There is, however, a further question I must now put to you. Was Martin Gee blackmailing you?'

'No, on my word, Inspector, no, no, no! I have not the faintest idea how he came by the cutting or why he kept it. Your questions are the first suggestion to me that anyone round here has ever known of my past. It's the first I've ever heard of it. You've got to believe me.'

A key was heard in the front-door, and Mrs Matthewson swept into the room.

'Oh, so sorry, I had no idea you had company, Julius.'

As she made to withdraw, her husband called her back.

'This is Detective Inspector Wickfield, dear, calling about Martin Gee's murder.'

'Oh, I see.'

'I was just on my way out, Mrs Matthewson. I may have to call back to ask you a few questions, but for the moment your husband has given me satisfactory information about the Christmas Eve party, and I shall bother you no further.'

Wickfield was inclined to believe Matthewson, slippery and ambiguous though he thought lawyers could sometimes be, but he made a note that he would at some stage need to ask Mrs Matthewson whether she could shed any light on the murder of Martin Gee. Mr Matthewson seemed to have a motive for removing Gee–if he was aware of Gee's knowledge of his first marriage–but Mrs Matthewson might have too. Or the couple could be acting in concert, for some reason not yet fathomed.

The inspector's next call was to the Linfords. The couple were at home, enjoying a late morning coffee in front of a cheerful fire. A small white poodle sat curled up on the hearth-rug. Linford was a florid man, in check trousers and an Aran sweater, spectacles perched on the bridge of his nose; a well-groomed individual, used to the power of money. His calling as an antiques dealer shone out of every article in the room: porcelain, prints, glass-ware, silver, pewter, art-work, furniture, it was all here in abundance. The inspector was sure the rest of the house would be similarly furnished. He imagined four-poster beds upstairs, carved blanket-chests, veneered wardrobes, a Chippendale washstand here, a Mawman long-case clock there. However, to business. Would the Linfords murder to protect their standing in the community? He wondered and determined to find out.

'Mr and Mrs Linford, you will not need me to tell you that I am here investigating the death of Mr Martin Gee. At the moment I have absolutely no hypothesis in my mind, so no one is to feel threatened. I am simply trying to find out what happened and pick up some pointers as regards motive and opportunity, you understand. Could I first of all ask you to remember back to the Christmas party. You were both there?'

'Oh, yes, Inspector. It is an annual event. That is to say, it is something of a tradition going back quite a few years now.' Mrs Linford continued: 'Drinks and a light supper on Christmas Eve, to prepare ourselves for the midnight service! Wouldn't be without it now.'

'Yes, my dear, but after this unfortunate circumstance, it might all feel a little different next year. We'll be wondering whose turn it is next. Sorry, Inspector, a tasteless little joke. Please go on.'

'Did Mr Gee put his glass down at any time and leave it unattended, do you know?'

'It's funny you should ask that, Inspector,' said George Linford, 'because one silly little detail is fixed in my mind. As we were going, I heard someone say, "Martin"–or it could have been "Mr Gee"–"drink up, we're off!". And I noticed that he picked his glass up from the top of the sideboard and quaffed it in a draught. Only a quarter of a glass, but it seemed a little out of character for such a - how shall I put it, Inspector?–such a fastidious man.'

'Was this voice male or female?'

'Male, I should say, but there was quite a bit of noise, and although I could see what Gee was doing, I was some way from the voice.'

'Thank you, Mr Linford, that could be very helpful. Now may I ask what were your own relations with Martin Gee?'

Wickfield saw both of them hesitate. Eventually George Linford spoke.

'We didn't take to him very much, did we, Robby? Not really our sort. Bit of a poseur, I should say.'

'I see. Have you any particular reason for saying that?'

Another slight pause.

'Well, for example, we had a disagreement over the authenticity of a picture, Gee and ourselves, and we discovered later that his so-called expertise in the field was a sham. At least in that area of modern art.'

'Do you know whether he had made any other enemies in this way–enemies determined enough to kill him?'

'Oh, I say, Inspector,' said Roberta Linford, 'we weren't enemies. We just didn't like him very much. We're not going out to kill anyone. As for anyone else, I've really no idea. Gee wasn't by all accounts very popular in the village, but there are no murderers in Halton Thoresby, I can assure you!'

'Perhaps you're looking in the wrong place, Inspector,' said Linford suddenly. 'Gee could have made enemies in other areas of life. For example, I happen to know that a certain married lady in this village, who shall be nameless, offered him, well, you know what, and he turned quite aggressive. Said she was making fun of his sexuality, that she was a nymphomaniac, that she was unprincipled, and so on.'

'Are you talking about Sa- ?' Roberta Linford broke off and bit her lip.

'Enough said,' hastily added Linford. 'We're not trying to drop anybody in it, Inspector, but I just wanted to suggest that art was not the only area in which Gee made himself unpopular in the village. But murder? No, I hardly think so.'

'May I just ask how you know about the incident you have just mentioned? Is it public knowledge?'

'No, Inspector, please forget it. I shouldn't have spoken. I was passing Gee's house one day when I overheard a conversation which was clearly not intended for my ears. I know nothing else against the lady in question which would suggest sexual predation, and it's got nothing to do with this case, I'm sure.'

As the inspector made his way back to the station, for a conference with his sergeant over a meat-pie in the canteen, he pondered the undercurrents of village life. The whole thing could have dropped straight out of Thomas Hardy: an apparently uneventful village, set in idyllic Worcestershire countryside, brimming over with sniping, sexually-charged emotion, mutual dislike, perhaps even murderous intent: human frailties in all their rawness. Oh, dear, this was not going to be an easy case.

VI

Pray, Goodman, please to moderate the rancour of your tongue!
Why flash those sparks of fury from your eyes?
Remember, when the judgment's weak the prejudice is strong.
Kane O'Hara, Midas, Act I, Scene 4

The inspector and his sergeant settled down to mushroom pie and chips and a pint of best bitter in the station canteen. The place was busy with people snatching meals or relaxing over empty plates, uniform and non-uniform, senior and junior, men and women. When they had satisfied the inner person, Wickfield invited his junior to open the batting.

'How did you get on with the worthy villagers of Halton Thoresby, Spooner? Any luck?'

'Well, Sir, Mrs Vickers was out shopping when I called, but I can't imagine she would have had much to contribute.'

'Don't you believe it, but we'll come to her later.'

'They're friends–*were* friends, I should say–of Martin Gee, remember. He was a regular guest at their annual soirées, and they saw him on several other occasions each year, apparently. Vickers' theory is that Gee took the heart stimulant–if that's what he used it for–unthinkingly, collapsed in the ditch on his way home and died of natural causes. He rules out intoxication–real intoxication–as a factor. On the other hand, he did eventually offer the information that Gee and the Linfords had had an acrid dispute about six months ago which left the Linfords considerably out of pocket, humiliated and angry–but not angry enough, according to Vickers, to lead to murder.'

‘OK, and the Simpsons?’

‘I’m afraid I got on the wrong side of Dr Simpson, so if we have another occasion to interview him, perhaps you’d do the job, Sir. Neither he nor his wife saw anything unusual in Gee or anyone else, either at the party or later at the church. They noticed Gee go up to receive communion but did not see him leave the church at the end. But the good doctor volunteered some significant information–because he realized we should find out anyway. Gee reported him to the GMC for mismanaging his treatment, and Dr Simpson admitted that Gee’s death was a relief because it means that the case against him cannot proceed. A reprimand, or worse, from the GMC, would have done Simpson’s local reputation no good at all.’

‘Do you see Simpson in the role of murderer?’

‘Possibly. We know he had opportunity, and of all people at the party he probably had easiest access to drugs. What about you, Sir, how did you get on?’

‘Like you, a mixture of the useless and the tantalizing. Because I know I’m prejudiced against lawyers, I did my best to be accepting and fair, and I found Matthewson quite a reasonable bloke. Civilized. Once I had confronted him with Gee’s newspaper cutting, he came clean and admitted that his present marriage is bigamous. He is terrified of the effect on his wife should she find out. He therefore, as I see it, has a very strong motive for murder, except that he claims he had no idea Gee knew about his first marriage, and he categorically denies that Gee had attempted to blackmail him. Difficult to tell at this stage. I’d need a little further persuasion before I cast our lawyer as a murderer, but I’m keeping an open mind.’

‘Can you think why Gee kept the cutting carefully if not for blackmail?’

‘No, not really. But that doesn’t mean to say he had ever used the information. He obviously suspected that Mattewson’s present marriage is not above board, and perhaps he was keeping the cutting by in case he ever needed a bit of help–financial, perhaps, or legal. I don’t know whether Gee would have made a ruthless enough blackmailer to benefit from his knowledge.

'Anyhow, I then called on the Linfords. Nice place, pots of money, what used to be called gentry. Now Mr Linford had one piece of information for us which might be useful. At the very end of the party, Gee had apparently placed his glass, a quarter full, on the sideboard, and as the imminent departure for the church was announced, he swallowed the contents hastily. This might explain why he couldn't taste any tampering with his wine and why, even if he had, he had no opportunity to mention the matter. Linford noticed that someone carefully drew Gee's attention to his unfinished drink, but Linford couldn't say for sure whether it was a man or a woman, and he couldn't say for sure whether the voice addressed Gee familiarly as "Martin" or more formally as "Mr Gee".

'Linford went on, at my prompting, to admit the row with Gee. Gee's pretence at expertise cost the Linfords near on £5000 but, more importantly possibly than that, it cost them standing with their friends. The Linfords clearly know a lot about antiques–that's their business–and no one can be expected to be an expert in all fields of art, but to be shown up to their friends as having made a major blunder in the purchase of a modern work of art would clearly not go down well with those so circumstanced. Would the Linfords take savage revenge? It would have to be revenge, because they couldn't hope to salvage any money from Gee's death; and in any case they're obviously not short of a bob or two. To avenge a slight might be sufficient motive to persuade them to murder Gee, but neither of them strikes me as a murderer. Perhaps that just shows how naïve I am.'

'You said something about Mrs Vickers earlier on.'

'Oh, yes. Roberta Linford, or really the pair of them together, let drop that Sally Vickers had made sexual advances to Gee and had been repulsed. They couldn't say whether the advances were made out of genuine sexual urge or, as Gee apparently thought, as a deliberate challenge to his virility, but they got the impression that Sally V. was humiliated at being refused: she had been slighted in her femininity! We may never know exactly what occurred if Mrs V. chooses to conceal the reality.

'However, we have other things to consider first. I want you to investigate Martin Gee's affairs: his will, his bank statements, his recent mail, that sort of thing, while I go to have a word with the vicar. After that, I suppose, for the sake of completion, one of us ought to interview the Matthewsons' guest at the party. Can't remember his name. He might have noticed something, though, and we'd–I'd–only come in for a reprimand if we left an obvious stone, however small, unturned.'

'Good afternoon, Vicar! Might I have a word with you about this unfortunate Gee business? We're routinely interviewing everyone who was at the Vickerses' Christmas party.'

'Yes, of course, Inspector, do come in. I'm not sure I can help, but I shall try.'

The vicarage was large and comfortable. Four or five rooms led off a large hall, and that must have meant four or five bedrooms upstairs, thought Wickfield. The lounge into which he was ushered was untidy but not chaotic. Piles of books lurched in all directions. Deep chairs invited the visitor to pick up a book and sink into the reading of it. A large print of St Michael's Mount hung above the fireplace, while French windows gave an enticing glimpse of a well-mown lawn leading down to a small stream.

'Now, Inspector, take a pew and fire away! But coffee first? My wife is upstairs resting, but it won't take me a minute to rustle up a cup of coffee.'

'No, thanks, Vicar. Not long had lunch, but don't let me stop you.' The vicar waved the suggested coffee away.

'What can you tell me about Mr Martin Gee that would shed any light on why someone should wish to murder him?'

'Well, I know he wasn't perhaps very popular in the village, but I don't know of any single individual who hated him enough to bump him off.'

The inspector was surprised at the reverend's choice of phrase.

'How well did you know him, if I may ask?'

'Well, Inspector, I'm afraid I cannot call Mr Gee a favorite member of my flock, and I admit, between these four walls, that I perhaps made less effort than I should to meet him as a pastor.'

'Could you tell me more precisely what you mean, Mr Thew?'

'Inspector, between you and me, I could not square his … tendency, if you get my meaning, and his profession of Christianity. It troubled me.'

'But surely you make a distinction between his tendency–his sexual orientation, I presume you mean–and his active life-style. He need not have been a practicing homosexual, you know.'

The vicar's prudish avoidance of proper terminology irritated Wickfield.

'Inspector, you can defend him all you like, but you will never get me to see that his … tendency was anything other than a blasphemy against the Creator. It is a demeaning, inhuman thing, expressly forbidden in the Bible.'

'I'm no theologian, Vicar, but I understood that the various biblical condemnations of sexual activity between males referred to pederasty, not to acts between consenting men.'

'Inspector, you are mistaken. The Old Testament is quite explicit.'

More than you are, my friend, muttered Wickfield to himself.

'But I thought the Old Testament was for the Jews, the New Testament for Christians. Did Jesus change nothing in human morality?'

'Jesus reinforced the injunctions of the Mosaic Law. Nothing that God lays down can ever be changed.'

'But, Vicar, Christians don't obey all the *ritual* injunctions of the Mosaic Law! They don't throw blood on the curtain of the temple, or force menstruating women to have a ritual lustration!'

'No, they don't. They very sensibly make a distinction between ritual and morality–which you would know, Inspector, if you had done as much study as I have.'

'But it can't be very easy to chop up the Law into ritual on the one side and ethics on the other. If all the laws came from God, how do you begin to distinguish?'

The vicar gave Wickfield a pitying look.

'In the Sermon on the Mount, Jesus re-emphasized the holiness of God's will, and St Paul interpreted him quite correctly when he called the human body the Temple of the Holy Spirit, dedicated to the one holy God.'

'What I don't understand, then, is that if Jesus brought nothing new in the way we perceive our relationship with God and with our fellow-humans, why don't we just stick with Moses?'

'Inspector, perhaps we should leave the discussion of these matters to weighty minds.' To weightier minds than yours, at any rate, Inspector, is what the vicar meant, thought Wickfield.

'In any case, Vicar,' Wickfield continued, ignoring the interruption in his peevishness at the vicar's assumed superiority, 'as you well know, there is no such thing as homosexuality: there are only individuals who are sexually attracted to members of the same sex. Did you not dismiss Martin Gee as a travesty labeled "queer" rather than as a human being with problems and aspirations the same as you and me?'

'Inspector Wickfield, I am sure you did not call here to question me on my pastoral methods. Are there other matters on which I can help you?'

There were not. The vicar professed himself quite unable to add any details from the party other than those already gleaned by the investigating team. Wickfield left the vicarage in an unhappy frame of mind. If the nation's churches were staffed by such dinosaurs, no wonder they were empty. Furthermore, could Mr Simon Thew's hatred of homosexuals, and hatred of one homosexual in particular in his own flock, have prompted him to take the grim reaper's scythe into his own hands? The inspector wondered. Rummer things than that were known to history.

Detective Sergeant Spooner headed for the bank shown on the check-book found in Mr Gee's house. The manager was in, he was available, he would be happy to help the police, particularly if it assisted, in however small a way, in the identification of a murderer. The manager's name was Wright, and he asked the sergeant to wait for a few minutes while the details of Mr Gee's finances, as far as the bank were concerned, were summoned from some unidentified inner recess.

After perusing the documents for a while, Mr Wright guided the Sergeant through them.

'So you see, Sergeant, Mr Gee had a monthly income which enabled him to live comfortably but not ostentatiously. A few small dividends are coming in regularly, royalties from his books, fees for consultancies. His outgoings are payments for utilities, rates, insurances and so on. Nothing remarkable. Competently organized. Each week he withdrew a small sum for current expenses–I take it–but the outgoings never exceeded the income.'

'You'll excuse this next question, Mr Wright, but you'll also understand that we are making wide-ranging inquiries in what is proving a slippery case. And I know that our conversation is confidential'–a slight question mark at the end of this sentence.

'Do Mr Gee's finances, in your opinion, give any evidence of receipts from blackmail activities?'

'Goodness gracious, Sergeant, that's a bit of a surprise. But the answer to your question is, No. All income is itemized and accounted for, as you see. There is absolutely no evidence of income from nefarious work. He could, of course, have had bank accounts elsewhere, of which I know nothing. But my knowledge of my late client leads me to accept that he had a modest income and lived within his means.'

'Would you care to put a figure on Mr Gee's worth, as at death?'

'That's difficult, you know, Sergeant, because to compute it you would need a knowledge of his life insurances, the likely value of his house, savings in building societies and the like. No, not easy at all.'

'Like to hazard a rough guess?'

'What you want to ask,' said Mr Wright knowingly, 'is whether it would be worth anybody's while to remove Mr Gee from the scene. As you are well aware, Sergeant, people have been known to kill for next to nothing, and added to that, the murderer may have thought–if he was after my client's money–that my client was worth more than he actually was. My quick assessment is that Mr Gee was not worth very much: £10,000, including the house, perhaps. Not enough, in my book, to risk a hefty prison sentence and the disgrace of a criminal record if a murder plan went wrong.'

Martin Gee's solicitor would be sure to have a copy of his will, if he had made one, and inquiries in Cannington revealed that the solicitor in question was Mr Button, the senior partner of Button, Clutton and Hutton. The will was produced, once Mr Button was satisfied as to the sergeant's *bona fides* and that of his inquiry.

'Can't be too careful, Sergeant: so many crooks around today, lurking in every crevice. Wouldn't do at all, no, not at all, to divulge confidential information to the wrong party. Of course, a will becomes public property once it is proved in court, but up till then it remains semi-confidential. I remember once–'

The sergeant cut him short.

'May we come to the matter of Mr Gee's will, Sir? That's the Mr Martin Gee, who died in Halton Thoresby on Christmas night. You doubtless read the account of his sad passing in the *Herald*.'

'Yes, my secretary informed me before you came that your inquiries concerned the late Mr Gee. Dearie me, what a tragedy, such a luminary in the artistic world. On one occasion, I remember–'

'Yes, thank you, Sir. His will?'

'Ah, yes, his will. I have it ready. Wouldn't do to keep busy policemen waiting, would it? As soon as my secretary phoned through, I ordered it to be brought up, on the likely chance that you proved to be genuine. If you had turned out to be an impostor, not only would you not have caught even the slightest glimpse of the will, but the police would have been waiting for you at the foot of the stairs to carry you off for further inquiries. We had a visitor once–'

'The will, Sir.'

'The will. Well, if we cut out all the legal jargon–the jargon is quite necessary, I may say, to avoid any sort of misunderstanding; you'd be amazed at the way the testator's wishes can be twisted and deformed in the hands of unscrupulous practitioners. We had a case once–but I musn't digress, must I? Your time is precious, I'm sure, and you don't want to listen to me blathering on. On the other hand, not only are some of these cases interesting in their own right, but they can shed light on present circumstances. Not in Mr Gee's case, I suppose, because it all looks straightforward to me, but you never know.'

'What does the will say, Sir?' Spooner found himself asking in capital letters.

'Martin Gee's will. Right. To the matter in hand. I drew it up, under his direction, about two years ago. Just let me look for the date.'

'WHAT DOES IT SAY?!'

'Mr Gee had only one living relative, a niece in Coventry–his late sister's only daughter. Everything goes to her, without conditions, with the exception of certain sums to named charities. I gather that the niece has been left comfortably off by her parents, but my client was anxious to keep things in the family as far as possible. Now, had he not had a niece–'

'Thank you so much, Mr Wright. If I could just have a note of the niece's name and address, I need trouble you no longer.' Phew. Prolixity seemed to be the ineluctable weakness of certain professions: lawyers and clergymen sprang to Spooner's mind, but it was by no means confined to them, as he was shortly to find out.

Detective Sergeant Spooner still had two visits to make that afternoon, with the late Martin Gee's doctor and with his accountant. He began with the latter, a certain Mr Garrow, whose name figured on documents in Mr Gee's desk. Mr Garrow was nearly as loquacious as the bank-manager, or would have been if the sergeant had not assured him that he would take up as little of his time as possible.

'Yes, Sergeant, I advised the late Mr Gee on the management of certain investments, but really all he wanted from me was how to avoid as much tax as possible. A perfectly laudable aim, of course, and one shared by all my clients. You may recall Will Rogers' dictum to the effect that "Income tax has made more liars out of the American people than gold has". Of course, I don't see my job as adding to the world's stock of lies, exactly, but at the same time–'

'Yes, I shan't keep you a moment more, Mr Garrow. Was there anything unusual about Mr Gee's income and tax affairs?'

'No, not at all, all perfectly straightforward. I found Mr Gee a little difficult to deal with–fussy, you know–but it is not my job to judge my clients, and in any case he never grumbled at my fees.' He uttered these words without a suspicion of self-mockery. 'Each year I must have saved him three times the money he paid me for my expertise. Don't think I'm boasting, Sergeant, it's just a matter of professional pride.' Sergeant Spooner, however, had already risen to make his exit.

Martin Gee's doctor, engaged, so to speak, after the disagreement with Dr Simpson, was a Dr Ronald Arbuthnot, who practiced in Bolham. He was a natty figure, with large round eyes and spectacles to match, who seemed to be perpetually bustling. His nails were long and well manicured, although red blotches on the back of the hand were less than sightly. The sergeant judged to him to be in his mid-thirties.

'Well, Doctor, you will have heard that your patient Martin Gee died on Christmas night, and I can tell you that he had apparently taken or been administered a strongish dose of digitalis. Had he a history of heart trouble?'

'No, Sergeant,' the doctor said, fidgeting with his tie. 'But he had more than once recently complained of a fluttering. I sent him for tests, but nothing was found. Bit of hypochondria, if you ask me.'

'So you didn't prescribe digoxin?'

'No, no, I didn't. But you know, if he was concerned enough about his heart, he could easily have made or obtained a drug for it: foolish, in my opinion, very foolish, but England is a free country–so far. I wouldn't *necessarily* be privy to any concerns of his over his heart.'

'Is there any other medical history that might have affected his ability to cope with a dose of digoxin or a few hours in the snow?'

'Well, Sergeant,' he said, scratching his ear and then twiddling his tie-pin, 'I really can't say until I know the dose of digitalis, the time at which and the circumstances in which it was taken, other medication he might have taken, and so on. But in general terms, no, he was a healthy man; just a bit of a fusser, that's all.'

The sergeant then returned to Martin Gee's house to embark on a more detailed examination of the deceased's desk, and for this he was joined by his superior. There was copious correspondence with editors of art journals and art books, concerning lay-out, contents, illustrations, references and so forth; letters from the niece in Coventry and a postcard from Germany from her; other letters from friends; the usual bills, marked in some cases 'Paid by direct debit'. In short, the desk yielded nothing. The detectives searched other furniture without turning up anything of note. They returned to the attic and turned out the contents of the boxes, and in particular of the black box. No death-threats, no poison pen letters, no accounts of vast debts, nothing to suggest criminal activity or criminal intent–except, perhaps, for the newspaper cutting they had already removed. There was the birth certificate, as they had left it. Martin Peter Gee, born 13 July 1905; father: Gerald Charles Gee, electrician, of Minehead, Somerset; mother, Monica May Spencer, factory-worker, also of Minehead, Somerset. Nothing peculiar there, one would have said (although one would have been wrong).

'Right, my lad,' said the amiable Wickfield to his sergeant after a time, 'we're getting nowhere fast here. Everyone at the Vickerses' on Christmas Eve seems to have some reason for getting rid of Gee, and yet none of them seems to me to be the material of which murderers are made. Yet one of them must be–I suppose. Of course, we may end up suggesting to the coroner a case of accidental death. There are still three people to be interviewed; and I also want to meet the people you interviewed, and you to meet those I interviewed. Perhaps our combined insights will enable us to narrow the field. Bit of psychologizing, you know. So this evening you will look up Mrs Matthewson, and I shall have a go at that wicked siren Mrs Vickers. Then tomorrow one of us can have a word with this niece in Coventry. Complete waste of time, I'm sure, but we can't afford to neglect a possible source of information.'

That evening, Detective Inspector Wickfield knocked on the door of Anchor Lodge, home to the Vickerses. He identified himself and was greeted jocularly by the man of the house.

'Ah, Inspector, I see we're now prime suspects: two visits from our detective team in one day! Makes me feel quite important.'

'Actually, Sir, it's really your wife I should like to see, since you've been so helpful to my sergeant already.'

Vickers shouted up the stairs, 'Sal, it's for you! A detective inspector, no less, to interview you!'

I could do without that sort of silly comment, thought Wickfield.

'Now, Mrs Vickers,' began Wickfield, once the two of them were seated alone in a small study at the back of the house. The noise of a television percolated through from the living-room.

'We have received information that you and the late Mr Gee had a difference of opinion, and we think this may have a bearing on the case. Would you mind telling me briefly what happened?'

'Do I have to? It can't have anything to do with the Christmas drinks, surely? And in any case, I'd much rather not talk about it, it was all so silly.'

'I appreciate that, Mrs Vickers,' the inspector said smoothly, in his kindest voice, 'but we feel that there could be a motive here for revenge out of pique or possibly jealousy, if your husband knew. I hope I am making myself clear. You understand that at this stage we are making no judgments, no accusations. We're simply thinking round the whole affair.'

'Look, Inspector, I don't know how you heard about this, and I can assure you that there was nothing in it. I was passing Martin's cottage one day, feeling bored. He was in the garden, weeding. I invited myself in and proposed a little–well, you know. He went nearly berserk. Started shouting and throwing his arms about. I excused myself rapidly and left in a hurry. And that was all.'

'May I ask whether you found Mr Gee attractive, Mrs Vickers?'

'No, not particularly. He was well past the first flush of youth, Inspector. But he was a man, and I thought it might be a bit of fun to tempt a, you know, one of those.'

Why were people in this village so coy?

'Were you very upset?'

'No, just a bit surprised at his reaction. Most men would, I flatter myself, have behaved quite differently.'

'Weren't you afraid the neighbors might have noticed?'

'Oh, no, it was well known that we were friendly with Martin, and my calling at his house in the middle of an afternoon would have occasioned no comment. In any case, I doubt whether the neighbors were even in, or, if in, awake.'

'Did the incident affect the way you thought about Mr Gee, or your conduct towards him?'

'No, why should it? You win some, you lose some. That's life. No point in getting worked up about it.'

The inspector wondered what it would be like to be married to someone like Sally Vickers. Not entirely restful, he surmised.

Meanwhile his sergeant was sitting at Ashton House, on the green, chatting with Mrs Deirdre Matthewson. The large dogs had been ushered into the kitchen.

'Is it you or your husband who reads Hegel, Mrs Matthewson?'

'Oh, my husband, Sergeant. My reading isn't up to that! Julius is a very well-read and intelligent man. I was so lucky to find him!'

'How long have you been married?'

'Twenty-seven blissful years, Sergeant. We married just after the war, when I was beginning to think I'd end up on the shelf!'

'Thank you, Mrs Matthewson. As you know, we're investigating the death of Mr Martin Gee, and we're interviewing particularly all those who were at the Vickerses' Christmas Eve drinks party. Can you think of anyone who might wish Mr Gee harm?'

'No, I can't. I didn't like the man very much, and I don't think my husband did either, but he was entertaining to listen to, and he was tolerated. I don't know of anyone in the village who would actually resort to murder. I can't of course speak for people outside the village, his wider acquaintances.'

'I think that's all for the moment, then. But I wonder whether you could tell me where I might contact your guest that night'– the sergeant consulted his note-book–'Mr Thornton Dismore.'

'Just let me look it up, Sergeant.'

She went to a bureau sitting against the wall and drew out an address book. 'Let me see. Dismore. Ah, here we are. Flat 4, Gilroy Mansions, Summerskill Road, NW3.'

'Thank you, Mrs Matthewson.'

VII

The crop-eared hound!
What the devil gave him the assurance
to purchase the inheritance of a family of four hundred years' standing?
Sir Walter Scott, A Legend of Montrose, Chapter VI

Nicholas Hotham was tormented by the thoughts of losing the Hotham estates (as he thought of them) to a jumped-up, tuppenny-ha'penny squirt from nowhere, with no weapon to brandish except a piece of paper (all right: three pieces of paper) from the eighteenth century, written in funny writing and in what might almost as well be a foreign tongue for all the sense some of it made. On the other hand, what if a genuine injustice had been perpetrated by his ancestors? He must get to the bottom of it, and that meant another trip to beard John Goode in his lair.

'Elisa, my dear,' he said one morning, after yet another night spent tossing and turning, 'I can't rest until I've sorted this out. Do you mind if I go to London again to try and reason with this bloke? If he is genuinely concerned that Joan Goode's will was twisted, whether through ill-will or through negligence, he should be willing to accept that we right the wrong by changing our name to Goode and displaying the Goode crest, perhaps on our note-paper. That way, Joan Goode's wishes will have been put into effect, even if a bit on the late side. If, on the other hand, he is a grasping, conniving *coglione*, I shall do my best to outface him. What do you say?'

'Oh, Nicholas, I don't know what to think, any more than you do. Another trip to London can't do any harm, can it? I'll look after the girls and keep things together here. Have you got enough pounds on you? Otherwise I've got plenty of lire you can change at the airport.'

One day therefore, shortly after Christmas–the 28th of December, it was–Hotham again found himself making the trip to London to see his tormentor, a fortnight after the bombshell that had upended his quiet life. This time he phoned Goode first, to make sure that his quarry would be in residence.

He took a taxi to the same seedy block of flats and mounted the same seedy stairs. Goode must have been looking out for him, because he was at the door of his flat, awaiting his visitor. There was an unpleasant smirk on his face.

'Mr Hotham, so good to see you again'–Christmas had eliminated none of his unction. 'I had not expected you quite so soon after your last visit–I wished to give you and your wife ample time to reach the right decision, you know–but you are very welcome, none the less. I presume you have come to accept my offer, and the sooner we come to business the better.'

Hotham was shown into the sitting-room, where a tray of tea-things was already prepared. He wondered idly where Goode had spent Christmas, because there was little sign of festivity in this exiguous flat. Perhaps he was not religious. Perhaps he had a mistress tucked away somewhere glamorous, whence he departed when the mood took him. What did he do for a living? And how had he stumbled on this will? At length, John Goode returned from the kitchen holding a tea-pot and a small plate of biscuits.

'Mr Hotham, it does me good to see you, because I feel in my bones that we are going to reach an amicable agreement today and that we can part the best of friends.'

I doubt that very much, you oily little man.

'Mr Goode,' began Nicholas, by way of reply, 'my wife and I have been discussing the situation, and we are prepared to go some way to meet you–if your explanations of our situation prove convincing. What if we change our name to Goode and display the Goode crest on our notepaper? That would satisfy the terms of Joan's will, as we understand it. Then we can arrange to transfer to you a quarter of our Yorkshire estates. Would that satisfy you?'

'No, I'm sorry, Mr Hotham. You see, to my way of thinking, your family, by its behavior, has forfeited the right to the estates: you no longer deserve to benefit from their rents. I should be doing Joan Goode a grave disservice if I simply let you and your lady wife continue to bleed the property.'

'"Bleed"? We look after the estate, we treat it properly. It is our patrimony, and we are proud of it.'

'Never the less, Mr Hotham, you must see the point I am trying to make. Because your forebears neglected, for whatever reason–I make no judgments on that score–to abide by the clear terms of the will, you have absolutely no right to any of the property. It is far too late now to try to make amends, in defiance of Joan's wishes. I could lay claim to the whole estate: I firmly believe–in fact, I know–I am the sole rightful living heir; but I am not a cruel man. I am prepared to leave you and Elisa–I may call her Elisa, may I not?–a moderate substance on which to start again.'

'You're not out to right an injustice or carry out the letter of Joan's will: you're out for your own gain!'

'As I see them, Mr Hotham, they amount to the same thing.'

'My wife and I'–no, you may not call her Elisa, you insignificant little man–'have discussed this matter at some length, as you can understand. We are prepared to offer you *half* the estate, in return for leaving us alone for ever after.'

'Mr Hotham,' began Goode slowly, 'I'm afraid you don't quite appreciate the situation. Will you permit me to present the facts to you, as I see them, in the hope that you may understand better where my interests lie? It will prevent any further misunderstandings between us. More tea?

'Let me take you back to the beginning, then. I want to put flesh on the bones of the family tree for you, to tell you what won't be apparent simply from looking at the pedigree. Adam Goode, where our story starts, died in 1538, age unknown, probably in his fifties. Who was he? I'm not sure: possibly a wool-merchant looking for extra work east of the Pennines. I have reason to believe that the family came from round Kendal, or possibly Cockermouth–but that's a detail over which we can argue later, if you have a mind to. The fact that his sons, as I explained, could not claim any notable ancestry when they obtained authorization to use the Goode arms officially in 1561 suggests that Adam was, in effect, nobody, a small man with the ambition to better himself. He married well, however: Katherine, a daughter of Lord Mitcham. They moved into Kellythwaite Hall, renting out the farm to a tenant. When he died, Adam left the farm and his business to his wife and then, after her death, to two of his sons, Peter and John. He was also able to leave a horse to his local vicar as payment for his prayers, but that is by the bye!

'His wife Katherine followed him to the grave after twenty-five years of widowhood. Her will shows that she had brought considerable lands with her into the marriage, and she now proceeded to leave them to her two eldest sons, James and Thomas. There were a whole number of smaller bequests: monies to the poor of the parish, funds for a "substanciall dynner" at her funeral, a colt here, a filly there, gifts to her servants, and so on. The bulk of the estate, however, was to go to her two eldest sons, and she added these words'–here Goode rummaged amongst the papers on a side-table–'sorry, just let me find the place. Ah, yes: " ... willing and monyng them as they estemye me lyving so after my death they love brotherlie and as they feare god, and treasure my blissinge, so they favor eiche other and never frowne nor disagree".

'Adam's and Katherine's two oldest sons lived into old age and into the next century. It was they who commissioned the family coat of arms, as a sign, presumably, that they had arrived at some social status which required recognition. Altogether Katherine and Adam had four sons and three daughters, but at this stage we are interested only in the eldest sons. We shall return to the youngest later.

'The eldest son James married a girl from a village nearby, and their eldest son Francis (1561-1617) inherited. Unfortunately, or fortunately, whichever way you look at it, James' wife Joan died after giving birth to seven children, and James then married a rich widow, Grace, who had two children by her first marriage. Grace's daughter Dorothy married her cousin Francis (son of James and Joan), and her son Robert married his cousin Elizabeth (daughter of James and Joan)–nothing quite like marrying cousins for keeping money in the family!

'Francis and Dorothy had sixteen–yes, sixteen!–children, with resonant names like Marmaduke, Leonard and Prudence. Some contracted good marriages: for example, the eldest, Thomas (1580-1643), married Mary Dewerton, the Dean of Durham's daughter, John married the granddaughter of a baronet. Another son became vicar of Acaster, and so on. Incidentally, when Mary died in 1633, her husband erected in her memory a remarkable tomb in the church at Callerton which you can still visit. It is in a chapel which contains the Goode arms, I might add. Thomas and Mary's eldest surviving son and heir was another James (1628-1694), who went to Cambridge University and became a lawyer. He brought more money into the family by marrying Frances, a baronet's relict, whose son by her first marriage wrote memoirs in which he described his new step-father as "a handsome gentleman" who treated him "with all civility and respect". This James became a JP, Deputy Lieutenant of the county and so forth.

'James' son and heir was another John (1660-1738), and it is through him, in a roundabout way, that the Hotham connection arises, which I shall come on to in a minute. John became an MP, donated a silver mace to St Mary's Hull and raised money for the restoration of that church etc. He made two advantageous marriages. His first wife Mary was a baronet's granddaughter and bore him two sons. His second wife was a baronet's widow and bore him a son and three daughters. One of his daughters, Constantia, married a local lawyer called James Burton, and we shall have occasion to return to him shortly. Let us go back now, though, to John's son and heir, Colonel James Goode (1688-1751). I have

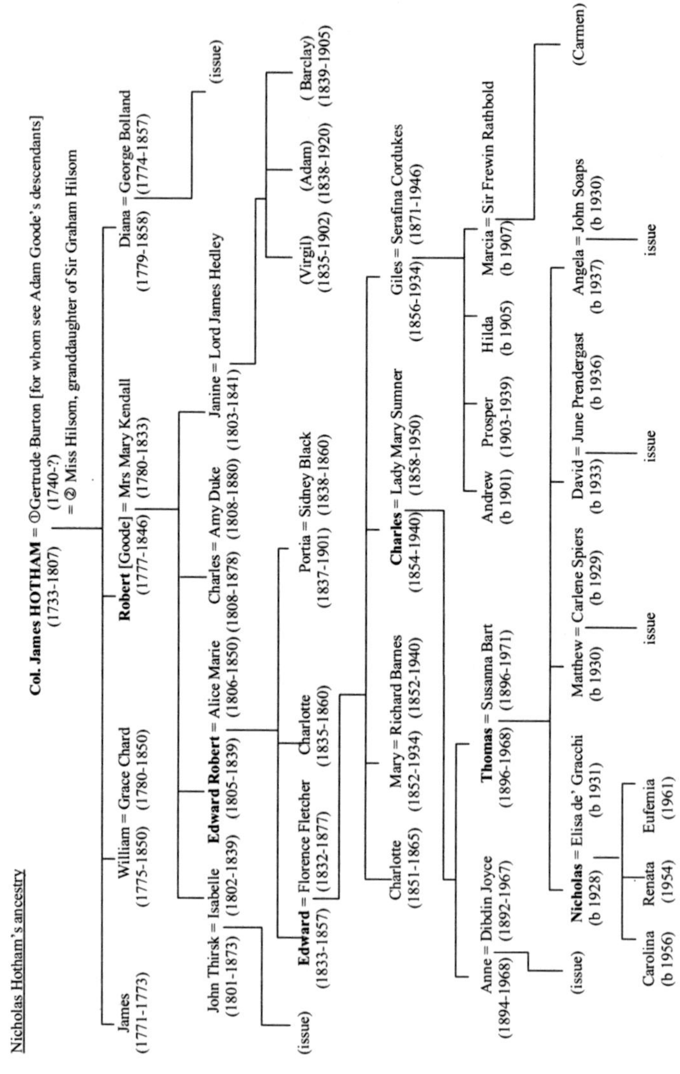
Nicholas Hotham's ancestry
Col. James HOTHAM = ①Gertrude Burton [for whom see Adam Goode's descendants]
(1733-1807) (1740-?)
= ② Miss Hilsom, granddaughter of Sir Graham Hilsom
James (1771-1773)
William = Grace Chard (1775-1850) (1780-1850)
Robert [Goode] = Mrs Mary Kendall (1777-1846) (1780-1833)
Diana = George Bolland (1779-1858) (1774-1857)
(issue)
John Thirsk = Isabelle (1801-1873) (1802-1839)
Edward Robert = Alice Marie (1805-1839) (1806-1850)
Charles = Amy Duke (1808-1878) (1808-1880)
Janine = Lord James Hedley (1803-1841)
(issue)
Edward = Florence Fletcher (1833-1857) (1832-1877)
Charlotte (1835-1860)
Portia = Sidney Black (1837-1901) (1838-1860)
(Virgil) (1835-1902)
(Adam) (1838-1920)
(Barclay) (1839-1905)
Charlotte (1851-1865)
Mary = Richard Barnes (1852-1934) (1852-1940)
Charles = Lady Mary Sumner (1854-1940) (1858-1950)
Giles = Serafina Cordukes (1856-1934) (1871-1946)
Anne = Dibdin Joyce (1894-1968) (1892-1967)
Thomas = Susanna Bart (1896-1968) (1896-1971)
Andrew (b 1901)
Prosper (1903-1939)
Hilda (b 1905)
Marcia = Sir Frewin Rathbold (b 1907)
(issue)
Nicholas = Elisa de' Gracchi (b 1928) (b 1931)
Matthew = Carlene Spiers (b 1930) (b 1929)
David = June Prendergast (b 1933) (b 1936)
Angela = John Soaps (b 1937) (b 1930)
(Carmen)
issue
issue
issue
Carolina (b 1956)
Renata (1954)
Eufemia (1961)

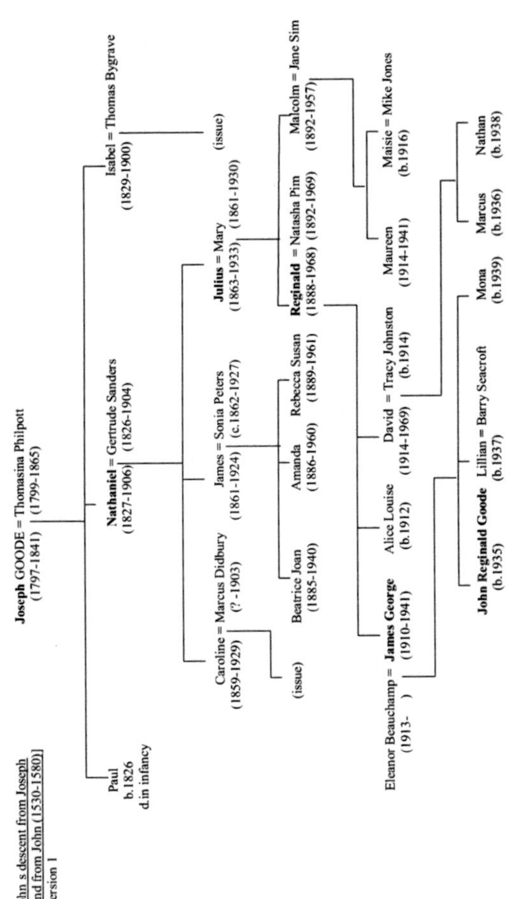

John s descent from Joseph
[and from John (1530-1580)]
Version 1
Joseph GOODE = Thomasina Philpott
(1797-1841) (1799-1865)
Paul
b.1826
d.in infancy
Nathaniel = Gertrude Sanders
(1827-1906) (1826-1904)
Isabel = Thomas Bygrave
(1829-1900)
(issue)
Caroline = Marcus Didbury
(1859-1929) (? -1903)
James = Sonia Peters
(1861-1924) (c.1862-1927)
Julius = Mary
(1863-1933) (1861-1930)
(issue)
Beatrice Joan
(1885-1940)
Amanda
(1886-1960)
Rebecca Susan
(1889-1961)
Reginald = Natasha Pim
(1888-1968) (1892-1969)
Malcolm = Jane Sim
(1892-1957)
Eleanor Beauchamp = James George
(1913-) (1910-1941)
Alice Louise
(b.1912)
David = Tracy Johnston
(1914-1969) (b.1914)
Maureen
(1914-1941)
Maisie = Mike Jones
(b.1916)
John Reginald Goode
(b.1935)
Lillian = Barry Seacroft
(b.1937)
Mona
(b.1939)
Marcus
(b.1936)
Nathan
(b.1938)

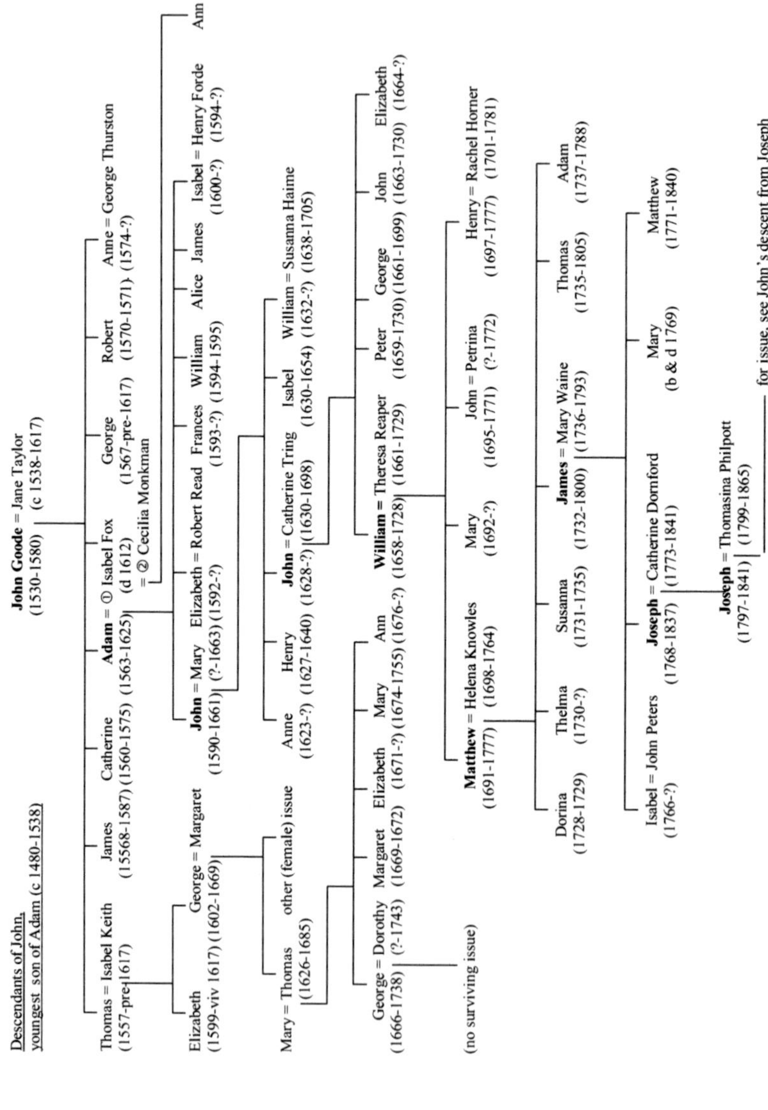
Descendants of John, youngest son of Adam (c 1480-1538)
John Goode = Jane Taylor
(1530-1580) (c 1538-1617)
Thomas = Isabel Keith
(1557-pre-1617)
James
(15568-1587)
Catherine
(1560-1575)
Adam = ① Isabel Fox
(1563-1625) (d 1612)
= ② Cecilia Monkman
George
(1567-pre-1617)
Robert
(1570-1571)
Anne = George Thurston
(1574-?)
Elizabeth
(1599-viv 1617)
George = Margaret
(1602-1669)
John = Mary
(1590-1661) (?-1663)
Elizabeth = Robert Read
(1592-?)
Frances
(1593-?)
William
(1594-1595)
Alice
James
Isabel = Henry Forde
(1600-?) (1594-?)
Ann
Mary = Thomas
(1626-1685)
other (female) issue
Anne
(1623-?)
Henry
(1627-1640)
John = Catherine Tring
(1628-?) (1630-1698)
Isabel
(1630-1654)
William = Susanna Haime
(1632-?) (1638-1705)
George = Dorothy
(1666-1738) (?-1743)
Margaret
(1669-1672)
Elizabeth
(1671-?)
Mary
(1674-1755)
Ann
(1676-?)
William = Theresa Reaper
(1658-1728) (1661-1729)
Peter
(1659-1730)
George
(1661-1699)
John
(1663-1730)
Elizabeth
(1664-?)
(no surviving issue)
Matthew = Helena Knowles
(1691-1777) (1698-1764)
Mary
(1692-?)
John = Petrina
(1695-1771) (?-1772)
Henry = Rachel Horner
(1697-1777) (1701-1781)
Dorina
(1728-1729)
Thelma
(1730-?)
Susanna
(1731-1735)
James = Mary Waine
(1732-1800) (1736-1793)
Thomas
(1735-1805)
Adam
(1737-1788)
Isabel = John Peters
(1766-?)
Joseph = Catherine Dornford
(1768-1837) (1773-1841)
Mary
(b & d 1769)
Matthew
(1771-1840)
Joseph = Thomasina Philpott
(1797-1841) (1799-1865)
for issue, see John's descent from Joseph

found out more about Colonel James than other members of the family because he became a prominent citizen of Hull and a well-known amateur architect, some of whose country houses survive to this day. He married a young woman called Sarah Dimmer, but unfortunately they left no male heir to carry on the name. Their son William died in infancy, and their other five children were all girls. Two of these girls died in infancy, two married well, and the eldest surviving girl, Joan, is the one whose will constitutes the foundation of my hopes and with the contents of which you are now familiar.

'What can I tell you about Joan? Unfortunately very little. She was born in 1720 in Hull, but when her father died in 1751, she moved to London to be near her sister Diana–I think–and there she died in 1796. She lies buried in Westminster Abbey, but I'm not quite sure why! She never married.'

Despite himself, Nicholas was interested in this account of the Goode family, which was entirely new to him. He sipped his tea, listening intently.

'And so,' continued Goode, 'we come to the Hotham connection. I have already told you–and you can see it for yourself on this pedigree–that the eldest of John (1660-1738) and Catherine's three daughters married a Beverley lawyer called James Burton. James and Constantia Burton had five sons, none of whom left issue, and a daughter Gertrude. Gertrude married a Colonel James Hotham as his first wife; he was Irish but lived in Devon. Gertrude, born in 1740, and Colonel James Hotham, seven years her senior, had three sons, James (1775-1853), who inherited the Hotham family house in Devon and had numerous children; William; and Robert. I haven't found out much more about William, but I know that Robert (1777-1846)–your great-great-grandfather–married a widow called Kendall and had a son by her, Edward Robert–your great-grandfather, of course. So the man who came into the Goode fortune and estates through Joan Goode's will was Joan's step-aunt's grandson, a quarter Goode. The only Goode blood in his veins came from his grandmother Constantia. Constantia was Joan's aunt by her grandfather John's second marriage. I, on the other hand, was born Goode, and I shall now tell you how.

'If we go back to Adam and Katherine of Kellythwaite, I mentioned that they had seven children. While their son Peter seems to have taken on the family farm at Kellythwaite, their youngest son John was set up as a farmer in a neighboring village and prospered in a quiet way. He married a local girl called Jane Taylor, and by a curious twist, Jane's mother Isabel married John's elder brother Peter! Anyway, John and Jane had numerous children and numerous grandchildren, and I can show you a tree in which I am the eldest male Goode descended directly from John through the senior surviving line. That puts me, I'm afraid, more directly descended from Adam than you are.

'Do you want to know what lessons I derive from this long story?' said Goode at length. 'For three hundred years the family pulled themselves up by their bootstraps, bettering themselves in each generation, extending their property and their influence, marrying well, keeping the estate together as a viable and prospering entity. Suddenly it all came to an end, through no fault of their own, because the last male in the senior line could not produce a male heir. Joan found herself a wealthy woman, owner of a worthy surname, an ancient coat of arms and a large estate but no one to leave them to. The codicils to the will demonstrate that her benevolence spread to embrace her servants and their families. Dressed up with nowhere to go, as you might say. She had one nephew, her sister Diana's boy, but he was not, of course, a Goode. Having moved to London forty-five years before, she had completely lost touch with junior members of the family, but her will makes it clear that, if no junior members could be found, a remote relation should be invited to shoulder the family responsibility, with a clear condition. That condition was not fulfilled. But here in me we have a junior member of the family who *is* willing and determined to shoulder the responsibility. I am a nobody, I start with nothing, but I believe that, given the same sort of start in life as Adam had five centuries ago, I can increase the Goode patrimony and enjoy the sort of success the old family did. Your lot have done nothing but mark time with it for the last two hundred years, consolidating but not increasing, soft-pedaling, avoiding risk, because things are easier that way. You don't deserve it.'

'Mr Goode,' said Hotham, 'how can you be so sure that the Hothams did not observe the conditions of the will? Do you *know* that they dropped the surname Goode?'

'Yes, I do, Mr Hotham. I have various bits of evidence, but it is here that the Bologna evidence becomes particularly important. The Hotham tombs in the Protestant cemetery in Bologna demonstrate, beyond a peradventure, that, while Robert died as Goode in 1846, his son Edward, who predeceased him, died in 1839 as Hotham, and so did both Edward's son Edward (1833-1857) and his daughter Charlotte (1835-1860). Part of this is clinched by another tomb in the same cemetery, that of young Edward (1833-1857)'s wife Florence (1832-1877): she too was buried as Hotham. And of course, if I may say so, you, Nicholas Hotham, are the definitive proof that the family didn't change its name!'

Goode and Hotham sat there for a while in silence, at the conclusion of this little speech. Then Goode spoke again.

'There are, of course, professional genealogists, people who spend their time in archives and libraries, poring over documents in a variety of scripts, people skilled in ancient usage and language, people whose medieval Latin is as fluent as your Italian or my French. Genealogy is also, however, accessible to the interested amateur, perhaps with a bit of assistance from the professionals. So, for example, the Borthwick will sell you a kit for coping with medieval and renaissance handwriting. Most of the ancient documents are available if you are prepared to travel and to wait. And I have put a lot of effort into developing my hobby. I was particularly pleased to have my work accepted for the archives of the Society of Genealogists. Now I know that they can't vet every piece of research, but it must have satisfied them to some extent.' Here he fell silent.

'Mr Goode,' said Nicholas, 'I'm not yet in a position to challenge your findings. If you won't agree to going 50/50 with us, my wife and I have decided to let the matter go to court. We can't afford to give up 75% of our wealth. If we take you to law, we may lose everything, but there is a chance of confirming our title and putting our ownership beyond doubt for ever. We therefore defy you to do your worst!'

Goode sat impassively for a few moments.

'I'm sorry, Mr Hotham. You still haven't understood the situation.' He paused, as if to let his words sink into Hotham's consciousness. He then spoke slowly.

'I know that in the first years of your marriage you had a brief liaison with a young Finnish girl and that you have an illegitimate son called Jacob, now aged fifteen. I'm quite sure your wife and daughters do not wish to be told about this. This is what makes genealogy such an interesting pastime.'

Nicholas rose in his chair. 'That's blackmail!' he almost shouted.

'No, Mr Hotham. I am merely applying a little pressure to encourage you to appreciate which side your bread is buttered. I am determined to have 75% of the Goode estate, and the arms, so that I can place myself legitimately in the line of my great forebears and carry their rich inheritance onward.'

Hotham had collapsed into his chair. He was pale.

'How did you find out?'

'The registrar made a mistake. He entered Jacob's surname as Goode before crossing it out and substituting the mother's name. Jacob's middle name is Nicholas.'

'Why didn't you tell me this at the beginning, instead of letting me think an accommodation might be possible?'

'Mr Hotham, believe me, I was unwilling to bring up a matter which I thought you might find painful. You have forced my hand.'

Nicholas looked drawn in defeat. How was he going to face Elisa and the girls with the news that three-quarters of their income was about to disappear? He hated this leering little man in the chair opposite him. He felt like strangling the miserable life out of his weedy body.

VIII

No Will-o'-the-Wisp mislight thee.
Robert Herrick, The Night-Piece, line 5

'We don't seem to be getting very far, Spooner, my lad. All the locals are suspects, and it's difficult to choose between them. None of them looks like a murderer to me at this stage, so suppose we try our foreigner, Mr Thornton Dismore? Can't do us any harm. Why don't you write up all our information so far–you never know, something may strike you–while I whiz up to London to see our Mr Dismore–checking with our local boys first, of course?'

The following morning, therefore, Detective Inspector Wickfield caught an early train to the Big Smoke and knocked on the door of Flat 4, Gilroy Mansions, Summerskill Road, NW3. No reply. Another knock, this time a bit louder. Still no reply. Drat: all this way for nothing. Why can't people be in when they're wanted? A well-dressed gentleman appeared on the landing, on his way downstairs.

'No one there,' he volunteered.

'No, I've just been knocking.'

'No, I mean the flat's empty just now. New tenants moving in tomorrow.'

'Are you the landlord, by any chance?'

'I am. Cecil Thistlethwaite, at your service'–this with a mock bow.

'When did Mr Dismore leave?'

A shadow crossed Mr Thistlethwaite's well-shaven features.

'May I ask who wishes to know?'

'DI Wickfield, Sir, from Worcestershire CID.'

He produced his badge.

'Working on a murder investigation, so I'd appreciate your cooperation.'

'Of course, Inspector. Had to make sure, you know. So many rogues about. Sorry, you would know about that better than I would! Mr Dismore left just before Christmas–the 21st , I think it was. Said he was going to stay with friends in the country.'

'How long had he been here?'

'Six months exactly. He paid for a six-month tenancy, cash on the nail. Said it was just to tide him over until he left for–abroad somewhere, Africa, was it? Can't exactly remember. Pleasant bloke, no trouble. Didn't see him very often, to be honest. I never had a complaint from the other tenants, money up front, can't ask for more than that, can you?'

'Did he leave any address?'

'No, said he wasn't sure where he'd be settling. In any case, he said, he got very little mail–which was true enough, and none of it was important, he said.'

'I couldn't just check inside the flat, could I, in case he's left a forwarding address anywhere?'

'No, help yourself.'

Mr Thistlethwaite fumbled on a bunch of keys, selected one, opened the door and said:

'Just close the door after you, will you, Inspector? It locks itself behind you. You won't mind if I get on? I shall be downstairs, in Flat 1, if you *should* need me.'

'Thank you, Mr Thistlethwaite. I don't anticipate any further questions.'

The flat was small–very small. The front-door led straight into the main room. Off this were a bedroom and a bathroom. Cooking facilities were available in a corner of the main room. Apart from a chest of drawers in the bedroom, a sort of welsh dresser in the living-room, a table on which sat a tiny television set, and a few chairs, there was no furniture. The 'dining-table' was a shelf that folded down from the wall. A few cheap prints.

Characterless. Oppressive. Still, people had to live where the work was. What had Dismore done for a living? 'Something in banking,' had someone said? Well, now he might never find out. The flat was quite empty, nowhere to hide anything. There was no sign of any paper giving a forwarding address or a telephone number. It was as if Mr Dismore not only was not, but in fact had never been. None the less, the Inspector gave the flat a thorough inspection. You never know … And although he did turn up a little something that might prove to be of interest, before sharing it with his sergeant he thought he needed to know a little more about the elusive Mr Dismore. Back to Halton Thoresby, therefore, for a talk with Mr and Mrs Matthewson.

'Mr and Mrs Matthewson, I'm glad to find you at home. Still very cold this evening, don't you think? Mind if I come in?'

The couple were clearly surprised, and perhaps a little unnerved, particularly Julius, to see the inspector again so soon, but they took his coat, ushered him into the living-room and sat him down before the fire.

'A drink, Inspector?'

'No, nothing for me, thanks, if by "drink" you mean alcohol. But a cup of tea would be welcome.'

'Certainly, we were about to make one ourselves. Now what can we do for you?'

When they were all settled in front of the fire, and three steaming cups of tea stood on as many tables, the inspector began.

'It's about your Mr Dismore. He seems to have disappeared, and I had got the impression that he was staying with you for some time, perhaps until after New Year. Apparently not.'

'No, Inspector, he suddenly announced on Boxing Day that he would have to be off, he hoped we'd excuse him, it had been such an enjoyable stay, he'd remembered things he had to do before he sailed for Africa. And he was gone. Drove off shortly after morning coffee.'

'How well did you know him?'

'Well, actually, not very well at all.'

'May I ask how you met him?'

'I can tell you exactly,' said Mrs Matthewson. 'In late July, Julius and I had a ten-day holiday booked in Cyprus–Limassol. We had already reserved half-way through the holiday a cruise to the Holy Land. You sail overnight on the first night, land and sight-see during the day, and then return on the second night. It's cheaper if you book with the travel firm beforehand. There's a sailing every day, I believe. We had a lovely time. Not too hot–just enough breeze, and although Jerusalem was crowded, we saw what we went to see. Mind you, I'm not sure I believe all the tourist blurb about "This is where Jesus was born"–how on earth can anyone know?–"This is the field in which the shepherds were keeping their flocks"–you know the kind of thing. All made up to keep the tourists happy. But we had a good lunch, good food on the boat and lots of entertainment. I liked the comedian best.'

'Mr Dismore, Mrs Matthewson.'

'Oh, sorry, got quite carried away by my memories. Thornton was a passenger on the boat. It turned out that his whole holiday exactly coincided with ours, only we hadn't seen him in Limassol at all until the cruise. We found him quite entertaining. He was by himself, seemed a bit lonely, and we invited him to share our table that second evening on the boat.'

'Yes,' Mr Matthewson took up the story. 'For the next few days in Cyprus we hired a jeep, the three of us, and knocked about the island a bit. Lots to see. Great history, lovely sea views. Then when we parted at Heathrow on our return to Blighty, we exchanged addresses and said we hoped we'd see him again.'

'What address did he give, can you remember?'

'A flat in London somewhere,' said his wife. 'The same address I gave your sergeant yesterday. Why do you ask?'

'Only to know whether there was any other way of getting hold of him. What sort of a bloke was he? What did he do for a living?'

Mr Matthewson again. 'Said something about banking, I seem to remember. Quite a modest fellow: could have been governor of the Bank of England, for all we knew. Seemed to have no friends, so we invited him up for Christmas. Said that usually he spent Christmas with a nephew and his wife–or was it a niece and her husband?–but this year they had decided to go abroad for a change, and could Uncle Thornton make other arrangements?'

'What did you talk about when you were together?'

'Oh, this and that,' said Mrs Matthewson, 'the usual things people talk about: television programs, the latest films, the weather, politics–you know the sort of thing.'

'What sort of a man was he, would you say? Educated? Right-wing? left-wing? Musical? Short-tempered? I need to fill him out in my mind.'

'You're wondering whether he's your murderer, aren't you, Inspector?'

'Not really, not at this stage. I went to his London flat earlier today, found he'd already left the country–but you knew that–and I was just curious to know whether he might have any useful information for us about the Vickerses' Christmas soirée–a detail he perhaps noticed and no one else did. Of course, we're still not totally convinced it's murder, but it's best to keep one's options open. I might as well ask you, though: did he strike you as murderous?'

'No,' said Mr Matthewson, 'but he was a little intense. Seemed always to be focussing on something other than what was going on at the time. Unsettled me a bit. He seemed to be concentrating on a matter outside our purview. If he'd been a witness in court, I might not have trusted his sincerity or his recollection. But maybe that's just me.'

'And,' added his wife, 'we'd taken it for granted he would be here for New Year.'

'We'd booked three tickets for the knees-up at Crackley Castle,' added Mr Matthewson, 'and then he announced out of the blue that he had to be off. Perhaps he thought he was next in line to be fed an unexpected narcotic. Sorry, Inspector, one of my silly jokes again!'

None of this was very conclusive or helpful, thought the inspector, but his sergeant might have come up with something. The two met in a pub, as detectives do, and they swapped information. The inspector first related his unsuccessful attempt to locate Mr Dismore and gave an account of his conversation with the solicitor and his wife. He added that there seemed something just faintly suggestive of mystery about Mr Dismore, from what the landlord and the Matthewsons were saying. He, the inspector, had a feeling he could not analyze that it would be worth getting to know Mr Dismore a bit better.

'Now, Sergeant, have you come up with anything?'

'Can't say I have, Sir, but to help me focus, I drew up a table of what we have so far. Do you wish to see it?'

'Of course, I do, my lad. That's why the police force employ you. But it will help me too.'

'As we know, all the guests at the Vickerses' party had opportunity to spike Mr Gee's glass. And as far as we can see, seven of them had motive–not very strong motive, perhaps, but you can't always be sure how feelings are going to affect people. So this is what we've got.'

name	**motive**
Mr Austin Vickers	?
Mrs Sally Vickers	repulsed in her sexual advances to Gee
Mr Julius Mattewson	Gee had incriminating information
Mrs Deirdre Matthewson	?
Rev Simon Thew	hated homosexuals
Mr George Linford	had suffered public humiliation over an art transaction
Mrs Roberta Linford	ditto by proxy
Dr Wartenby Simpson	Gee had reported him to the GMC for misconduct
Mrs Helen Simpson	would share her husband's fear of exposure
Mr Thornton Dismore	?
Martin Gee's niece	inherited a sum of money

'Thornton Dismore is an unknown quantity. I've added in Martin Gee's niece, because, although she wasn't at the party, she could have had an accomplice. Dr Simpson could be expected to be the one with easiest access to heart drugs. Mr Linford and Dr Simpson had suffered or would suffer professionally; Mrs Vickers' humiliation was more personal; Mr Matthewson would fear the effect on his marriage. The niece did not fear anything, but she stood to gain directly by her uncle's death. She does not seem to have been hard up. Who's to say which of these motives could lead to murder and which couldn't? So no, Sir, I haven't really got very far.' Spooner was a little disconsolate.

Wickfield thought about the sorry tatters of human life exposed by this table. Here in all its shame was the spectrum of peccadilloes, weaknesses and embarrassing secrets characteristic of one small village. Beneath the surface calm of Halton Thoresby, a village inhabited by the prosperous and the respectable, the contented and the successful, was a murky swirl of jealousy, rivalry, prejudice, incompetence, fear and irregular sexual appetite.

'Well, my lad, I may have something for you. When I was in Dismore's London flat, I didn't really expect to find anything, but tucked in between a water-pipe and the skirting board, just where it might have fallen off a table and disappeared unnoticed, I found a small card, about the size of a business-card. There was an address on one side of it which may just be where we can pick up the trail of Mr Dismore.'

'That card could have been there for months, or even years, Sir. What makes you think it can help us in our present inquiry?'

'Because on the reverse side were a few words in a scribble'– and he produced the card with a flourish out of his inside pocket– "*the* letter posted 11 Dec 1973: a date to remember!".'

'And what was the address, Sir?'

'Well, one of us has got a little trip coming up! It was'–and he turned the card over for the sergeant to read for himself– "Palazzo Gravina, via dei Polacchi, Roma". Sunny Italy, here I come! Except that it will be winter there as well as here! While I'm enjoying international travel, as befits my station in life, you could do worse than look up Gee's niece in Coventry.'

Grace me no grace, nor uncle me no uncle.
William Shakespeare, Richard II, Act II, Scene 3

Spooner set off for Coventry by the first available train, a short journey through some admirable countryside. The three famous and stately spires loomed up against the grey sky as the train drew into the station. (He understood that the station was quite a distance from the city centre–shades of Bologna!–because the city fathers in Victorian times were aghast at the prospect of steam–engines polluting their gracious townscape.) A short taxi-drive to the east of the city-centre took him to No.135 Bolingbroke Road, Stoke, just off what, in the nineteenth century, had been called Gentlemen's Green. A modest suburb, but quiet and conveniently situated between two main roads for easy access to the city centre. No city looks its best in early January, with slush on the roads and pavements and a dull sky lowering overhead, but the green was an oasis of peace and the houses along it dignified. Prudent telephone-calls the previous evening had ensured that Mrs Elsie Tucker was expecting him and that local constabulary toes were not being trodden on.

'Come in, my dear,' she said to the policeman standing on the doorstep. 'You must be Detective Sergeant Schooner. You're the one who phoned last night, aren't you?'

'I am, Mrs Tucker, but the name's actually Spooner.'

'Oh, well, never mind, it's not your fault, I daresay. Now I've just put the kettle on, as Bill and me was just going to have a mid-morning cup of tea. Always do, you know–when we're in, that is, not if we're out shopping, of course, except that then we pop into a caffe. You'll join us, won't you? A cuppa never did anyone any harm, despite what these medical boffins tell you about too much caffeine or whatnot. I take no notice of them, myself. Completely out of touch with reality, these people; don't know where they get their ideas from. They should come along here, and I'd soon tell them what's what.'

'You know your uncle died before Christmas, Mrs Tucker?'

'Oh, yes, dear. His solicitor phoned me the day after Boxing Day–a Mr Mutton, I think he called himself–or was it Sutton?–anyway this chap phoned to say my uncle Martin had passed on, and he was very sorry to have to tell me bad news, and the funeral would be in the New Year, and so on. He fairly went on, he did, about this and that, hardly giving me time to think.'

'Did he tell you how your uncle died?'

'Something about getting lost in the snow on his way home from church. What a daft thing to do!'

The conversation was suspended while Bill brought in a tray of tea-things.

'Hello, there, Sergeant. How do you do?'

Unlike his wife, who was small and almost dainty, Bill was an untidy piece of goods, apparently cobbled together from disparate parts in haphazard fashion, the whole surmounted by a mop of unruly hair. His clothes did not fit.

'Milk? sugar?'

When everyone was settled, Mrs Tucker began again.

'The solicitor wasn't very sure about details of uncle Martin's death. Can you tell me what happened, Sergeant?'

'Well, Mrs Tucker, your uncle attended a drinks party at a neighbor's on the evening of Christmas Eve. He went to the church for the midnight service, along with the rest of them, and at the end of the service he left for home alone and on foot. You know the road, the one that goes into Cannington. Only your uncle's row of cottages lies that way, and none of the two other families had been to the midnight service. It had been snowing quite heavily, and the roads were difficult. I doubt whether your uncle could have got a lift, even if he'd wanted one. He seems to have stumbled into a ditch within a few hundred yards of home and failed to get up again. His body was found next morning by a villager walking his dog, but by that time of course, as far as we can see, he'd been lying in the snow for perhaps seven hours.'

'Well, it's a shame the old boy had to go like that, all on his own, but I shan't grieve much, I'm afraid. We got along all right, but I can't say I was really very fond of him.'

'Bloody poofdah, he was, and all,' Bill muttered savagely.

'Now there's no need for that, Bill. He never did you any harm.'

'No, but what good did he do us, tell me that?'

'Mrs Tucker, can you tell me a little bit about your uncle? We're beginning to understand that some people, or a person, did not like your uncle, to the point of wishing to do away with him.'

'What do you mean?' expostulated the bereaved niece.

'I mean that there is some doubt about whether your uncle's death was an accident–if you get my drift.'

'You mean he was bumped off?' asked Bill.

'You could put it that way, Mr Tucker.' He turned back to Mrs Tucker.

'How? You just said he fell into a ditch and died of hypo-, hypo-whatever it is.'

'It seems, Mrs Tucker, and I don't wish to distress you in any way, that someone at the drinks party laced his last glass of wine with a heart drug. The effects did not make themselves felt until shortly after your uncle left the church, about an hour later. On his way home, he could have felt too drowsy to continue and just flopped down where he was. It's possible, of course, that your uncle had the drug himself, in his pocket, perhaps took it half-way through the service if he felt it would steady his heart up a bit, but seriously miscalculated the effect. The trouble with digoxin is that its effects are very unpredictable, which makes it a curious weapon to choose in a murder, in one way. We may never know, but at the moment we're just trying to eliminate the action of an enemy as a factor in your uncle's unfortunate death. The suspicious thing–well, two suspicious things, actually–is–are–that there was nothing in his pockets to contain digoxin tablets or tincture, and there was nothing in his home or garden to suggest he had been preparing the drug himself. And his doctor knows nothing about heart trouble in your uncle.'

'Well I don't like it at all. There are some nasty people about, if all they can think of doing is murdering harmless old men in the street.'

The sergeant had already noted that, in Mrs Tucker's estimation, sixty-eight was 'old', but he made no comment.

'Did your uncle have any enemies you know of, Mrs Tucker?'

'No, dear, I don't know–apart from Bill here, of course.' The sergeant took this to be a little joke and did not respond.

'My uncle never married, as you probably know, and he did not seem to have a wide circle of friends. This was a pity, because he could be quite good company. He had a fund of stories and could talk about all sorts of things.'

'What sorts of things, Mrs Tucker?'

'Well, dear, as I said, up till the war, I was too young to take any notice of silly adults' conversation, but when he came to stay with us after our marriage–you quite liked him then, Bill, didn't you?–he'd tell us about the war, he'd talk about his work as an art historian, about his travels in France and Germany, and as he got to know us a bit more, he'd talk about being lonely, about how difficult it was for "people like him" to get along in society.

'He'd tell us silly jokes, you know. One I remember went like this. A Catholic priest on pilgrimage in the Middle East one day decided to hire a camel to cross the desert. He approached a line of camel-hirers. "Ah," said the dealer, "you've come to the right man, because my camel is a very religious one." "How d'you mean?" asked the priest. "Well, it obeys only religious orders. To get him to start, you say *Deo gratias*, and to get him to stop you say *Ave, Maria*. That's all there is to it. Splendid camel." So the priest climbed on, got himself comfortable, offered a quick prayer to his guardian angel, and said "*Deo gratias*". The camel stood up and trotted off as good as gold. Soon the pair were racing across the desert at impressive speed.

'I can remember his tone of voice as he told us this story.' A small tear formed in the corner of her eye. She sniffed.

'After a while the priest noticed to his horror that crossing the horizon as far as the eye could see was a huge chasm and that they would tumble into it if he couldn't bring the camel to a halt pretty soon. He was dismayed to realize that he couldn't remember the right word of command. "Amen!" he shouted. "*Kyrie eleison! Pater noster*!" Nothing seemed to work. "Ah, I've got it: *Ave Maria*!" The camel slithered to a halt inches from the mouth of the chasm. "Phew!" said the priest, as he mopped his brow. "*Deo gratias!*"'

There was a suitable reaction from the detective.

'Was your uncle a religious man?' he continued after a while.

'Yes, I think so. We didn't discuss religion very often, you see, dear, as Bill's not that interested. Are you, Bill? When uncle Martin stayed with us, he made a point of trotting along to the parish church, just off the Binley Road, on Sunday morning, but he never talked about it very much. I sometimes wondered whether he saw religion as a substitute for marriage.'

'How often did you see him?'

'Too bloody often' was heard from the sergeant's right.

'You mean recently or when I was little?'

'Both.'

'Well, we used to live in Minehead, on the sea. My grandfather Gerald was a carpenter there, like his father before him, and my grandmother was a dinner lady at the local primary school. Martin was born in–let me see, it would be 1905. My mum was born in 1907. When my mum married, she moved away from the area. Met this bloke from Coventry and settled here. Uncle Martin used to visit us when I was a kid, in the 30s, couple of times a year, perhaps, coming up from Somerset by coach and staying a week at a time. I suppose he would have come more often, only my father wasn't too keen on him. Thought him a bit of a pansy.'

'Which he was' from the sergeant's right.

'Before the war–I was only seven in 1939–I was a bit young to appreciate him as an intelligent and thoughtful man. All I could see was his irritating mannerisms, his fussiness and what I would now call his camp manner. Then after the war, in my late teens, I met this gorgeous hunky fellah–'

''Ere, steady on!' said Bill.

'It's you I mean, you fool! And here we are. The war had put paid to uncle Martin's visits, for a while. Then in the '50s, after Bill and me was married, we used to invite him here. Mum was dead by then, you see. Bill didn't like him any, nor did I, really, but I used to feel a bit sorry for him, because he was all on his own'– 'No wonder!' chimed in Bill–'and in a peculiar way I got something out of his visits. We'd take days out, you know, the usual things, Kenilworth and Warwick, Brandon race-course and so on, we'd go to the flicks, we'd have a few walks. He'd pay his way, he wasn't a burden on us, and I'm sure he enjoyed coming. But I'm not really sorry he's dead, as we shan't have to put up with him again. Does that sound very mean?'

'It sounds perfectly natural to me, Mrs Tucker. After all, we don't choose our uncles, and there's no reason why we should necessarily be fond of them.' He did not wish to be sanctimonious, but he was not sure what else to say that would not sound unfeeling.

'Mrs Tucker, this may be a rather indelicate question, so don't answer it if you'd rather not. Did your uncle have any male friends–liaisons, I mean–which turned sour? Could he have had a lover angry enough to wish to kill him?'

'Bill and I got married in 1955. A lovely wedding we had, Bill, didn't we? All the family there, the full works in the church. Lovely.' She sat musing for a while. 'Where was I? Oh, yes, so when uncle Martin began to stay with us, he was already fifty. Perhaps his active sex life, if he'd ever had one, was over. I don't know. He certainly never told *us* about quarrels or personal difficulties in that way, did he, Bill? My father died in 1950 of a heart attack, and my mother in 1952, and they never talked to me about Martin's sexuality. Why should they?'

'What can you tell me about his professional life?'

'He spent a lot of time on articles for newspapers: he was the Arts Correspondent for a number of local papers. He spent time in libraries, researching his favorite painters, and he attended a lot of showings and exhibitions. He traveled abroad quite a bit, particularly in Italy. His real interest was seventeenth-century Venetian art, I think, but I was never really interested enough to ask. Couldn't name you a single Venetian painter if you asked me, I'm afraid. Not my thing at all.'

'Do you know whether he could have had professional rivals? Had he damaged anyone's reputation?'

'Sorry, dear, no idea. He was more or less retired. At sixty-five he said he was going to fold up his notebook: he'd had enough of traveling and working to editors' deadlines. This last year he didn't do much work at all. I can't see him having professional rivals anyway. What do you think, Bill?'

'Sorry, what was that?'

'Nothing. Just wondering. So I don't think we can help you much there, Sergeant.'

'Tell me, did you know you were the main beneficiary of his will, Mrs Tucker?'

'No, I didn't. How on earth do you know?'

'The solicitor told me.'

'How much do we get, then?' asked Bill promptly, who at mention of the word 'will' had suddenly woken up.

'Well, I couldn't take it on myself to say. The solicitor said he couldn't really put a figure on it. He thought perhaps about £10,000, including the house.'

'Would do us nicely,' Bill commented. 'We could do with that sort of cash at the moment.'

'Why do you say "at the moment"? I thought Coventry was all right–car manufacture, machine tools, man-made fibers, that sort of thing.'

'Well,' said Bill, 'things ain't what they used to be. I've worked at Alfred Herbert's for years, but I'm facing the axe. The work's drying up, they say. Looks as if I could be out of a job before long. On the scrap-heap at forty-three! I ask you, what's this country coming to?'

'Don't worry, dear,' consoled his wife. 'Even if you're made redundant, you'll get a severance package, and there's always work in a big bustling city like Coventry. We'll manage.'

'Your uncle's solicitor, Mrs Tucker, hoped you weren't short of money, because he says it may take some time for Mr Gee's estate to be wound up. You know how these things are.'

'We're not on the breadline, if that's what you mean, but a little help from uncle Martin would come in very handy. However, if it's not to be, it's not to be, and we'll have to manage. Shall we meet you at the funeral, Sergeant?'

'Yes, Mrs Tucker, I shall do my best to be there. Do you know anyone at Halton Thoresby who can give you and your husband a cup of tea afterwards?'

'Yes, we know uncle's neighbor, Miss Jennings. She's over eighty but still makes a lovely cup of tea. She'll be sorry to see him go, I know. They got on quite well, I think.'

Sergeant Spooner drew up his report in the privacy of the second-class railway carriage on the return journey. Martin Gee was not really any more popular with his closest relatives than he seemed to have been with his acquaintances. No known enemies. Nothing in his private or professional life that spelt obvious danger. People enjoyed his company, but in small doses. A seemingly harmless individual, who lived as he could, bothered few, entertained his readers for many years, contributed to humanity's stock of knowledge. Spooner found himself wondering about the assessment of personal worth. What made one individual worthier than another? And worthier to whom? He recalled the (probably spurious) series of graffiti supposedly seen in an Oxford public toilet:

'To be is to do'–Aristotle

'To do is to be'–Mao Tse Tung

'Doo-be-doo'–Frank Sinatra

Was it better to do or to be? Was there a difference?

Talking of Aristotle, the *Nicomachaean Ethics* was, he recalled from his schooldays, an attempt to map out what made a human person successful–successful not in social but in personal terms. To make the most of yourself, you needed to practice the 'virtues' or, in modern parlance, 'life-skills'. Spooner could not remember how many life-skills the philosopher listed: twenty? twenty-five? Was there not something missing from this picture, however? Could Martin Gee's life be satisfactorily assessed just on the basis of the life-skills he had acquired? Did his religion not give worth? And was the world worse off or better off for Martin Gee's passing? These were heavy questions.

Spooner was brought back to his present situation by the train's deceleration prior to the end of his journey. Did he see Bill and Elsie Tucker as potential murderers, keen to hasten the acquisition of whatever inheritance might come their way through her uncle's death? He doubted it, but his report could not definitely rule out the possibility. Yet more suspects. Oh, dear.

Forward, as occasion offers.
Never look round to see whether any shall note it [...]
Be satisfied with success in even the smallest matter,
and think that even such a result is no trifle.

Marcus Aurelius, Meditations IX, 29

Detective Inspector Wickfield had not visited Rome before. In fact he had not been to Italy. He and his wife often holidayed in Britain, but if they went abroad it was more likely to be to places not frequented by tourists than to a city that was the mecca of millions. Mind you, places unfrequented by tourists were dwindling by the year, he sometimes thought. The Wickfields might as well stick to the remoter parts of western Ireland or northern Scotland: nothing to beat a good stretch of Caithness! However, when a quick trip to Rome was offered on a plate, he was not averse to taking advantage, even though he had to leave his wife behind. As he flew out of Heathrow, he wondered what the connection was between a Roman palace and the death of unpopular Mr Gee in a little village called Halton Thoresby. Was he completely unbalanced, wasting tax-payers' money following a thread as thin as gossamer?

Despite a complete lack of Italian, he managed to get himself on the bus that led from the airport to the center of Rome. From the square in front of Stazione Termini, having no idea where to go next, he showed a taxi-driver the address for which he was heading. The cab sped off amidst a welter of horn-blasts and imprecations. Piazza della Repubblica, he read on the street-signs, Via Quattro Fontane, Via Sistina, Via della Croce, Via delle Due Macelli … Wickfield lost track of direction and settled back to enjoy the ride. It was cold but sunny, and the drive through these unfamiliar streets was stimulating. The predominant smell was fresh coffee: lovely! Eventually they came to a halt, and Wickfield handed over what he later found out to have been double the fare that the cabbie should have charged if he had come a direct route. Not to worry. Put it down to experience.

Cars parked haphazardly on the pavements made the attractive architecture of the street a little hard to appreciate, he thought. Palazzo Gravina itself had an imposing façade on the narrow street. Stucco work near the top was flaking off. Grids protected the ground-floor windows, but paint on the shutters higher up was peeling. Handsome, but in need of a face-lift. He rang a bell to the side of the wicket set in the grand double doors, wondering what he would say and how he would contact Mr Dismore if he were indeed lurking somewhere in this large building. Instead of a uniformed servant appearing at the door, a female teenage head poked itself out of a first-floor window and shouted down, '*Si? Chi è?*'

'*Buon giorno!*' he said. '*Parla inglese?*'

'Yes,' said the head. 'How can we help?'

'I'm looking for the man or the lady of the house.' That sounded a bit lame, but what else could he say?

'OK, I'll come down. Half a mo.'

"Half a mo"? What sort of English was that in the heart of Rome?

The person who appeared full height at the wicket announced herself to be Renata–'but everyone calls me Rena'. 'My parents are upstairs. Come in.'

A broad stone staircase swept up from the inner courtyard to a long corridor running down the length of the building. His guide led him to a heavy, decorated door which opened into a comfortable salon, wherein sat a lady and a gentleman reading newspapers. The man rose.

'Good morning,' he said. 'I gather from my daughter's speech that you are English-speaking.'

'Detective Inspector Wickfield, Sir, Worcester CID.'

'Well, well, Inspector, nothing wrong I hope? Come in, sit down. You're very welcome, whatever your business.'

The lady expressed a similar sentiment, with an accent.

'I'm not quite sure how to begin. May I first of all ask your name, Sir?'

'Yes, it's not a secret. I'm Nicholas Hotham and this is my wife Elisa. You have just met our middle daughter Rena.'

'Does the name Thornton Dismore mean anything to you?'

'No, not a thing.'

'Martin Gee?'

'No, nothing.'

'Madam?'

'No, nothing, sorry.' The 'th' came out like a 't', and the 'g' lingered.

'May I ask how long you have lived here?'

'Since always. That is, this palace has been in the Gracchi family for generations, and my wife and I moved in on our marriage eighteen years ago. Why?'

'Mr Hotham, I am carrying out what we think is a murder investigation. One of the witnesses has disappeared, but in his London apartment I found a card with this address on it'–and, producing the card from his pocket, he handed it over to the bemused Hothams.

The couple exchanged a significant glance.

'Inspector, we have recently had dealings with a man from London who announced the start of our–connection–in a letter posted from London on 11 December. But his name was Goode, not Dismore.'

'Do you know anything about this man Goode?'

A pause. Nicholas looked across at his wife, who nodded.

'Inspector, I'm going to tell you the whole story, and then you can decide for yourself whether there is any connection between our troubles and your murder. The letter from Goode to which I referred claimed to be based on an eighteenth-century will in the name of Joan Goode. This lady, of genteel family, who died in the 1790s, left all her money to the Hothams, who were distant relations, on condition that they changed their name to Goode. This apparently they never did, or at least insufficiently to satisfy the condition as worded. They continued to call themselves Hotham but took over the Goode's Yorkshire estates, and have continued to live on the profits of the estates ever since. What with dwindling rents and higher costs, the income now keeps us solvent, but we don't have much to spare–as you can see from the state of the house! The letter went on to claim 75% of the estate as the rightful property of a genuine Goode, namely himself, the writer.

'Anyhow, we received this letter on 14 December, and on the 15th I flew out to London to see what on earth was going on. We were both of us not just puzzled but quite upset by the letter. I had a long conversation with John Goode, and I didn't take to him at all. He said that 75% of the estate was his price for leaving us in peace. He took me through some family trees to convince me that he had the law and justice on his side. He gave us a month in which to think things over. If we rejected his offer, he would take us to court, and, as he pointed out, we could have our ownership confirmed by the court, or we could lose everything. It was a dreadful dilemma to be in, and I came away even more depressed than before.

'Elisa and I discussed the matter endlessly, as you can imagine. We even took the children into our confidence. We eventually decided to let the law take its course and examine Goode's evidence. Before that, though, we would make an offer of 50% of the estate to get Goode off our backs.

'Accordingly, on 28 December, two days ago, I again flew out to London and saw Goode. He was as smarmy as before and irritatingly condescending. He rejected our offer, repeated that he was holding out for 75%, and we could take it or leave it.'

With a slight blush on his cheeks, and studiously avoiding his wife's face, Nicholas omitted the revelation that Goode had made to clinch his bargain.

'I left him with the promise to contact our York lawyers as soon as possible in the New Year. Elisa and I have agreed that we must give up 75% of the Yorkshire estate, and that I adopted the only course available to us.'

'Excuse me a moment, Sir, you said earlier that you had agreed to accept Mr Goode's challenge in the courts. What made you change your minds?'

'We decided eventually that we would rather keep 25%, our good name–excuse the pun–and our peace of mind. A court case, with probable appeals, could have dragged on for years, and we were unwilling to put our daughters through that. So we have capitulated, and the lawyers will now sort out the details. I shall look for a job here in Rome, so that we can maintain this house, and Elisa is also hoping to earn an honest income.'

'What do you know about this man Goode? Did he tell you anything about himself?'

'No, he didn't, Inspector, but I drew some conclusions from his flat. He is clearly an educated man, because some of the books on his shelves were high-brow. His flat is neat and well-furnished, but in a rather seedy area. He tried half-heartedly to convince me of the existence of a wife and a son, but I somehow didn't believe him. The section of his bookshelves devoted to genealogy was impressive, but perhaps its bulk exceeds its quality. I wouldn't know. His intensity seems to come from a fixation with the Goode family, all five hundred years of it.'

'What sort of age? Appearance?'

'Late thirties, perhaps forty, something like that. Neatly but not expensively dressed. Medium height, mousy hair, brown eyes, clean shaven, non-descript sort of face, average build. Sorry, I'm not being much help, am I?'

'Can I see the will and the family trees he gave you?'

Nicholas went over to a writing-desk, pulled the lid down and extracted a small sheaf of papers.

'I made copies so that I could take them with me on the plane for purposes of closer scrutiny, and you're welcome to have these. What connection do you think there might be between your murder case and this wretched will?'

'I've no idea, Sir, I'm afraid, but quite a lot of money is involved in the Goode-Hotham confrontation, if you'll pardon the phrase, and where there's money, there's motive for murder. Can you give me a few minutes just to take a quick look at these, in case I've any further questions for you at this stage?'

He took the sheets of paper, settled back in his chair and read through them. He looked at the reverse of the last sheet to make sure he had missed nothing.

'Hmm,' he commented, 'our Miss Goode seems to have been a redoubtable lady. Why on earth should she forbid someone to go to India? I wonder whether there is anywhere a portrait of this lady–perhaps seated with a poodle on her lap, her hair heaped on top of her head, an aristocratic expression on her thin features and gold jewelry dripping from her clothes? A female version of Trollope's Sir Harry Hotspur, perhaps. All this talk of stewards and house-maids and servants has given our friend John Goode ideas above his station, I think. Anyway, I'll take these papers away with me, if I may, and give them a closer look. Then a visit to Mr Goode might be advisable. In the meantime, Mr Hotham, can I ask you not to proceed further with your lawyer over this business, not until I've sorted out the other end of this affair, if I may so phrase it, and I'll get back to you as soon as possible? Have you a phone number for a quick contact?'

'Look here, Inspector,' said Mrs Hotham, 'you can't get a convenient flight to London this evening–you'd never get out to the airport in time, for a start–so why not spend the night here? We're going to a performance of *Traviata* at the opera-house in a while, and I'm sure one of the girls won't mind giving up her ticket, if the opera interests you.'

It was agreed that Wickfield would postpone his departure until the morning. Despite the excellence of the evening's performance, Wickfield was no nearer a solution to his riddle when he landed back in London the following day. He sat at his desk to view the documents with meticulous attention. He read through the will. He scrutinized the Goode family trees, and the glimmer of a thought began to dawn in his mind. Finally, after some hours, he summoned the sergeant and announced that he now knew who Thornton Dismore was, and he was beginning to see why Gee had been murdered. All still conjectural, but it was a hypothesis to keep them going.

'Yes, Sir,' said Sergeant Spooner expectantly. 'Who is Dismore, then? Come on, don't keep me in suspense.'

'Right, Sergeant, turn first to the list of villages in which the Goode properties lie, according to Joan's will. It occurred to me to look up on a modern map the whereabouts of the estate, starting from the principle that an estate is likely to be as compact as possible: not scattered over a whole county, but concentrated in a smaller area of the county. Now the lands mentioned in the will are clustered roughly in a triangle between Malton, Pocklington and Strensall. Some of the villages mentioned have changed names since the will was drawn up in the eighteenth century. For example, Laythorpe is now Layerthorpe; Sunderlandwick is now two separate places, Sunderland and Wick. And do you know what Aike is called today? Credit this if you can: *Thornton* Aike! Not bad, is it? Next, go to the family tree of the senior Goode branch. Joan Goode is shown as the last of her line, without brothers or male cousins. This is why, of course, she resorted to such a curious will. You will see that her mother's surname is Dimmer.'

'Yes, Sir. So?'

'Spooner, my lad, according to a book I have consulted, Dismore is simply a variant of Dimmer: the same surname, but in some families it appears as Dismore. In short, our friend Thornton Dismore is a species of spirit that arises out of Joan Goode's will. He is, in a word, John Goode, disguised so that Mr Goode can adopt another identity to fool his victims. What do you say?'

'Bit of a long shot, Sir, if you don't mind my saying so.'

'We'll lodge it in our minds as a probability, although we can't yet exclude completely the possibility that Thornton Dismore exists in his own right.'

'And what about Martin Gee? You said you knew why he had been murdered.'

'I didn't say I *knew*: I just said I was beginning to say a glimmer of light. Martin Gee was "Mr G."–"G" for Goode! In other words, he too was a Goode, and he stood in the way of John Goode's inheritance. How's that?'

'God bless me, Sir, you may be right at that! How are you going to prove it?'

'I'm not: you are! You will start researching Martin Gee's ancestry.'

'So what's your hypothesis, Sir?'

'Right, as I see it, this is how things went. Goode takes up genealogy. Don't know when or how, we may find out later, but it doesn't matter at this stage. In the course of his researches, he comes across the will of a distant ancestor which seems to promise him a small fortune. The seeds of an idea are implanted in his mind. His researches further reveal that he is the oldest male member, bar one, of a junior branch of the family and has a good chance of verifying his claim to the satisfaction of a court of law. The family who gained the inheritance are still using their original surname, in defiance of the will. Unfortunately for John Goode, there is this other member of his family who takes precedence: a cousin, shall we say, who stands in his way, insurmountably. John Goode conceives the idea of eliminating this cousin surreptitiously and then coming forward unchallenged to claim his inheritance. He knows where this cousin lives, under a modified form of the name, and befriends a fellow-villager to give him unsuspected entry to the cousin's circle. He parades under a false name, Thornton Dismore, to allay all suspicions of kinship and to be able to disappear afterwards with no fuss. He proceeds to poison the cousin, or administer a heart drug which leads to his death, and then quietly disappears. Without any apparent connection to this murder, he steps forward in London, far from the scene of his crime, in his own name of Goode, and claims the Goode estate. His one mistake so far, as I see it, is to have dropped a small card measuring 1 inch by 2 inches which puts us on his track, as we have seen. How's that?'

'Why doesn't he simply go to court instead of settling for only 75% of the estate? You'd have thought the risk worth his while, particularly if his genealogical evidence is as solid as he claims. And the court would have eliminated any doubt as to his contentions, so that he could sleep contentedly in his bed at night.'

'No, I think not. An experienced genealogist appointed by the court, let us say, to investigate Goode's claims, would very soon have uncovered this cousin. Goode, you notice, has suppressed all suggestion of another claimant in the trees he gave to Hotham. Much of all this is conjecture, but it gives us something to start on and put flesh to. It's high time we paid a visit to our Mr Goode, so we'll travel to London the day after tomorrow, when the trains are running again, and that'll give you time to start your research! Let us hope Mr Goode does not prove as elusive as his friend Mr Dismore.'

In the meantime, Spooner set to work, and, with a bit of assistance, was able to come up with the following story. Martin Gee's parents were a certain Gerald Gee and Monica née Spencer. They had married in 1903, in Minehead where they were then living, and their only son Martin was born in 1905. No problems there. Gerald's parents were Roger (1850-1917) and Hilda née Plumsted (1851-1953), still in Minehead. Roger was a carpenter, and Hilda ran a small sweet-shop. They made a passable living. The trouble was with Roger's father Paul (1824-1899). Paul was a fisherman in Grimsby, with his own boat that he ran with his brother Nathaniel. During a storm in January of 1879, the year before Roger was born, Nathaniel was lost overboard. There was gossip that Nathaniel had had his eye on Paul's young fiancée, Anne Wilkins. Nathaniels' death was treated officially as an accident, all too common unfortunately amongst the fishing community, and so forth, but the whispers about a possible helping hand into the sea from his brother would not die down. It is not known what Anne thought about the 'accident', but eventually the couple decided to up sticks and start afresh. They moved to Minehead, where they married and set up as Mr and Mrs Gee, fisherman and fisherman's wife. They gambled that no one would connect them with an accident in the North Sea–and they were probably right. Their son Roger was registered as Gee, without question, since in this Christian country of ours, parents may, in most circumstances, call themselves and their offspring what they like, without a by-your-leave from interfering officials. So the family became officially Gee, and no one the wiser. Paul's parents, Joe and Thomasina, knew of the change of name, but doubtless agreed for the sake of their son and his new wife.

'Remember,' interjected Wickfield, 'most people don't go back beyond their grandparents. Very few have known their great-grandparents or, if they have, been old enough to question them on their past. I bet most people couldn't even name for you their great-grandparents or identify their great-grandmothers' maiden names. It's possible Martin Gee never knew his surname was originally Goode. Not that that knowledge would have helped him.'

Spooner continued with his story. Goode had caught up with these facts because Paul went down on Roger's birth-certificate as Goode. So Paul Goode from Grimsby, fisherman, reappeared as Paul Gee of Minehead, fisherman, and it did not take genius to make a connection. It was even easier for a watchful genealogist like John Goode, because he knew of family members in Grimsby who had not changed their name, including his own grandfather, and of Gees in Minehead almost into the present day. His intuition would have been helped by the tendency at the time for families to remain in one place: moves away from a family centre wreak havoc with a genealogist's work, particularly if the name is not an uncommon one. When the police caught up with Goode's own researches, matters might be even further clarified.

On 2 January, therefore, DI Wickfield and DS Spooner traveled up to London, second class, to question a suspected murderer. It was a murky day. The snow had turned to slush; the sky was overcast and drab. Most people not at work seemed to have stayed at home, probably with their feet up, very sensibly, and the two detectives were able to make their way rapidly from the railway station to Goode's flat. They climbed the same seedy staircase that Hotham had climbed twice the previous month and knocked imperiously on the front-door of Flat 33. No reply. Damn. Not another empty flat, surely? Try again. Still no reply.

Had their bird flown? Were they just too late? And yet how could he have got wind of their visit? He had not been warned by Hotham, had he? That would complicate their inquiry. The inspector felt that a more aggressive measure was required, and with the assistance of a suitable implement from the local police-station, in the absence of anyone they could find claiming to be the landlord, entry was gained. The smell was not pleasant. There at his table was John Goode, as large as life–but unfortunately not quite so natural. He lay sprawled forward, his head on his arms. On the table in front of him was an empty tumbler and a bottle of Manerix. Under his arm was a piece of paper, containing just two words in an almost illegible scrawl: *Mea culpa.* The gas fire was still alight, on low. The flat did not seem to have been the target of a search: no disorder in the sitting-room, at any rate. A quick inspection of the other rooms in the flat bore no surprises. The bed was made; the towel in the bathroom was folded on the rail; a small amount of crockery and cutlery in the kitchen was stacked ready for the washing-up. No signs of other occupancy. The atmosphere told them, however, that Mr Goode had been dead for more than a few days. The detective inspector would stake his reputation, whatever the appearances, that John Goode had not committed suicide.

XI

To heirs unknown descends the unguarded store,
Or wanders heaven-directed to the poor.

Alexander Pope, Moral Essays, Epistle 2, lines 149-150

Standard police procedure ensured that photographs in abundance were taken, the flat examined for finger-prints, signs of forced entry searched for, before the inspector and his sergeant were able to make a thorough examination of the flat. The air was sweeter, and the two were able to work systematically in comfort. Their only source of useful information, however, turned out to be the living-room, and in particular the section of the bookshelf devoted to genealogy. This testified to the owner's abiding interest in the subject which had led him to snatch at a fortune.

The detectives sifted through the books, box files and papers, and realized that most of it would not lead to the identification of a murderer–if there was one. There was one box, however, which promised richer rewards. The outside carried the enigmatic label 'F3P6', and the contents were to occupy their entire evening. It transpired that John Goode was a long-standing member of an international organization called, for brevity's sake, F3P6. The box contained his membership details, such as date of entry, subscription paid, membership number, and contact details of the leadership. A flier advertised the aims of the organization.

F3P6

In 1949, a Swiss aristocrat named François Peyerolle de Montmorillon conceived the genial idea of initiating a foundation to assist members of noble and wealthy families to retrieve their name, titles, properties and estates from the hands of the peasantry into which they might have fallen after the havoc of two world wars wreaked in Europe. He gave his foundation the sturdy and enlightening title of *Fondation pour la Pûreté, Préservation et Promotion de Familles Prestigieuses*, or F2P5, which, with his own initials, produced F3P6–snappy and memorable. As the Foundation extended its work, centres were set up in the United Kingdom–*François Peyerolle's Foundation for the Purity, Preservation and Promotion of Prestigious Families* or F4P5–Germany–*Stiftung für die Reinheit, Konservierung und Förderung von prestigeträchtigen Familien* or SRKPF3–and Italy–*Fondazione per la Purezza, Preservazione e Promozione delle Famiglie Prestigiose* or F3P6, but in the interests of uniformity and comprehension, all affiliated member-cells are asked to maintain the unique nomenclature F3P6.

To qualify for assistance, applicants have to satisfy the Board of the following conditions:

1. they have a realistic chance of recovering lost estates (or name or title etc)
2. their claim is genealogically sound
3. their present income is insufficient to achieve their aims
4. they undertake to abide by the methods of restitution decided on by the Board.

On the basis of a non-returnable registration fee, members receive help in a number of useful directions: finance, advice, access to libraries and archives either in person or by proxy, and contact with past members.

The rationale behind F3P6 is simple and should claim the adherence of all right-thinking members of Europe's élite. The Founder, who died in 1963, believed that progress, whether social, political, philosophical, technological, artistic or other, rested on the shoulders of the cultivated and intelligent few. He based his findings on a long list of families and dynasties which, he found, had contributed more significantly than individuals, however brilliant, to the rise of modern Europe, for example the Bourbons, the Medicis, the Rothschilds, the Plantagenets, the Tudors. His work *Progrés en Europe et la Contribution de certaines Familles Importantes,* is now available in six languages and is offered to F3P6 members at a generous discount.

For further information, or to contact the Board, please write to the M.le Secrétaire, F3P6, Poste Restante, Geneva.

This flier seemed to announce a shadowy, if not exactly sinister, foundation, and Wickfield was anxious to discover more. If Goode were a paid-up member and had exploited its services, could he have fallen foul of the leadership, perhaps by threatening to reveal illegal activities or contacts or by failing to abide by any conditions of membership? To his satisfaction, the box-file contained a copy of Peyerolle de Montmorillon's work in English translation, and it fell open at a page marked by Goode with a piece of card. This is what it said:

States have not always fairly acknowledged the contribution of aristocratic families to the State in the maintenance of order, in the promotion of well-being, and in the development of new ways of thinking, but have regarded them as rivals to the supreme power or as deviations from a narrow norm or–perish the mark!–as élitist. Yet it is precisely those qualities which seem a threat to some that, properly managed, ensure the continuance and prosperity of the State. I refer to the stability that comes with inherited wealth when invested in property and land, the accumulation of insight and wisdom that accompanies the careful nurturing of genetic purity, and the wider concern for the well-being of Society which is closed to those whose daily grind concentrates their attention on mundane tasks.

This contention is supported by the Roman Catholic Church in its promotion of family life and its recognition that the individual is subservient to the requirements of the wider unit. For example, in his Apostolic Exhortation *In familia fidens*, Pope Eugene V quotes the venerable St Jerome: *Sancta et fidelis domus unum sanctificat infidelem. Candidatus est fidei, quem filiorum et nepotum credens turba circumdat* [One unbeliever is sanctified by a holy and believing household. One who is surrounded by a crowd of Christian sons and grandsons is a candidate for the faith, *Epistula cvii, I*]. Or again, in his address *Nell'Ordine della Natura* [In the Order of Nature] of 1951, Pope Pius XII says:

In the natural order, among social institutions, there is none which the Church has closer to her heart than the family [...] The family itself has always found and will always find in the Church its defense, protection and support in all that concerns its inviolable rights, its freedom and the exercise of its lofty function.

Other religious bodies teach that the family is a source of good. We read, for example, in *The Book of Mormon*: 'And again, the Lord has said that: Ye shall defend your families even unto bloodshed' (Alma 43.47). The holy *Koran* has the following injunction: 'You who believe, protect yourselves and your families from a fire whose fuel will be men and stones, in the charge of stern and mighty angels who never disobey God's command' (Surah 66.6). In the Jewish scriptures, we read that 'G-d lifts the poor man clear of his troubles and makes families increase like flocks of sheep', or, as another translation has it, 'But now, he lifts the needy out of their misery, and gives them a flock of new families' (Psalm 107.41). This list could be extended indefinitely, because all the world's great religions have prized the family as the building-block of society.

This is not in any way controversial teaching, and we should like to go one step beyond it. History teaches that families which rise to the top in stable societies such as those characteristic of Europe in the last millennium are those which combine essential virtues with the determination to preserve and strengthen them. It is no use possessing virtues if those virtues die out for want of encouragement. To excel in matters of statecraft or warfare or mercantile effort or conquest, and yet not to ensure that these skills are handed down to the next generation, is criminal neglect. How can humanity prosper and go forward if its greatest treasures are not husbanded from age to age? The science of genetics shows that, more often than not, skills are inherited, not acquired. To be more accurate, skills are not acquired by those who have no aptitude for them inherited from their forebears.

We see it as our duty, therefore, to foster the growth and temporal persistence of families who have shown, through their deeds and effects, that they are capable of carrying Society forward, acting as a force for good by imposing on it the highest values perhaps underappreciated by lesser members.

There then followed a passage which Goode (presumably he) had marked with double red lines in the margin, as being worthy of particular notice:

Of course, families fall on hard times through no fault of their own. Circumstances may be stronger than genetic inheritance, and it happens that the inherited treasures fall into unworthy hands, or that the potential that is present fails to develop because war, or misfortune, or financial failure, or untimely death or any one of scores of other historical factors beyond the individual's control, wrest management of the genetic resources out of the hands of those most capable, *ceteris paribus*, of furthering them. In these cases, our response should not be indifference: that would be to surrender to the forces of barbarism and entropy. Our response must rather be to succour the afflicted, to raise up families that have fallen, to stand solid with those whose continuance is threatened.

Wickfield was bemused. He was no scholar, but he thought he recognized twaddle when he saw it. This tarradiddle of half-truths, quotations wrenched out of context, innuendo and slipshod logic was surely the meanderings of a crackpot: how could anyone be seduced by it? If, however, the F3P6 was still in existence after twenty-four years, something must be striking a chord somewhere. He read on:

The recent science of genetics–recent in the sense that the foundation laid in the last century by Mendel and Bateson is only now yielding exciting results–has pointed up the importance of purity in the genetic line. Of course, inbreeding–the reliance on an insufficiently wide genetic base–is pestilential and achieves the opposite of its intentions, but we advocate not inbreeding but selective breeding. In other words, genetic material with a proven record of success should be matched with material of equal value. This second material may stem from families whose success has been modest in actual terms but whose potential is clear. We leave it to the experts to determine more closely what the criteria for this might be, but an Appendix to the present work carries some of our own thoughts on the subject. We stress, therefore, that the purpose of any genetic program of value is not simply to maintain the present level of success but to raise it. Families with intense social application are to be encouraged to increase their effectiveness by searching out members of other families in combination with whom the progress so far achieved can be extended and improved.

Wickfield thought he had read more than enough to satisfy himself as to the drift of the author's argument. Goode clearly read this stuff. The heavens preserve us. The inspector moved on to consider other literature in the box. There were pamphlets by members of F3P6, newspaper cuttings about various European families of note, magazine articles about the wealthy and successful (self-made millionaires figured prominently)–and a document taking further the program announced by the flier he had read earlier. It said, amongst other things:

The new member of F3P6 will wish to acquaint him or herself thoroughly with the methods of the Foundation. Generally speaking, we are committed to legal means of attaining our ends, but where national or international law is demonstrably ineffective or unjust, we reserve the right to advance with means on which some might frown. The member will therefore be strongly advised to withdraw his or her candidature for membership before proceeding further with the submission of the immediate problem to the Board. In order to obtain documents that are not available in recognized collections such as public and private libraries and state archives, it may from time to time be necessary to employ the services of someone with developed entry skills' [for which read "burglar", thought Wickfield]. 'Similarly, to remove the threat of reactionary resistance, it may from time to time be necessary to employ the services of a discreet agent whose sensibilities do not extend to avoidance of all violence' [for which read "assassin"] 'although in general terms we deplore the use of force. It should be clearly understood at the outset that members are required to accept in writing the strategy decided on by the Board for the furtherance of the member's purpose. There is always ample opportunity for consultation and discussion. In the contrary case, betrayal of the Foundation will not go unpunished.

The inspector sat back to ponder what he had read. His assistant had been working through other material, and his first duty was to share with Spooner the gist of what he had read about F3P6. Spooner was aghast.

'How do you think Goode got himself into this, Sir?'

'Can't imagine. On the other hand, the Foundation seems to advertise itself a little indiscreetly, perhaps through political societies or gentlemen's clubs. Some of the publicity must be by word of mouth. However, no one would bother with it unless there was a fertile soil in which the seed could take root, so we can't blame Payroll, or whatever his name was, for peddling this pernicious stuff. There are probably a number of ways in which Goode could have come into contact with it. The point is, he seems to have committed himself to a course of action which, one, put him within reach of his goal but which, two, involved the elimination of a rival–if I am reading the evidence correctly. He contacted the Foundation, outlined the problem and admitted, presumably, to having insufficient funds to do the necessary research. For example, if he wished to tap the resources of the Borthwick Institute in York, or the County Records at Northallerton, he would have needed to travel and to stay in Yorkshire for the duration of his researches. Consultation of old wills and parish registers is a time-consuming business: you could spend hours leafing through documents and end up with a single reference that you then have to fit into your other work. Goode would probably have had to follow courses in the reading of medieval handwriting, perhaps also in the peculiar Latin of the church and the law. He might have had to go abroad in search of relevant material. The organization might also offer to help with legal fees in the event of a court case, but as we have seen, Goode was probably reluctant to go to court. The reason must be the subject of our next investigation.'

'Where did he meet the F3P6 Board, do you think?'

'Probably here in London. Any UK headquarters is going to be here, I should think. But probably his meeting with them took place some time ago–years, I've no doubt, because one doesn't amass this amount of material in a few weeks. Goode had an inkling that a small fortune had fallen into the wrong hands–we may discover how he found this out when we take a closer look at his genealogical work–and he uncovered enough evidence to make his own claim plausible. He then approached F3P6 for financial help and perhaps advice: genealogy is a tricky science, and O-Level English and O-Level Latin are inadequate preparations.'

'It follows that other people know of Goode's murder of Gee.'

'Ah, we don't know he *did* murder Gee, my lad. That's only supposition on my part. But you're right: if a crime has been committed, it is known to others–probably. On the other hand, when it came to the point, he may have decided to act on his own–safer that way, you see: no witnesses, no threats of divulgation, no one to come along afterwards and force him to share the profits. So let's have a look for his immediate family tree: that's where I think he rubbed out Martin Gee in thought before rubbing him out in reality. But you've got me at it, now. Goode is innocent of Gee's death until a court of law finds him guilty. Bit late for that now, of course, but we can hope to produce the evidence that would have convicted him if he had lived. If he was guilty, of course! Musn't be condemning the reputation of innocent people to death by false verdict, must we?'

Wickfield and Spooner searched on, and it was not long before they laid hands on the document for which they were looking. Sure enough, there was a significant column which had been expunged from the version of the Goode/Gee family tree that John Goode had handed to Nicholas Hotham. Four generations of Goodes descended from Joseph's elder son Paul (1824-1899) were listed, placing Martin Peter Gee as the eldest living(!) Goode, senior to John's own father James. A sister for Paul had been added to the defective tree, perhaps to disguise the gap, perhaps because she really existed. A genealogist appointed by a court to research the sanitized tree could have checked on the birth (or baptism, more likely) of Paul Goode in 1824 at Grimsby, but no record of his marriage or death would be found, and 'died in infancy' would be as good a guess as any, even without the evidence of a burial in a parish register. In any case, without further information derived, for example, from family tradition, he or she would not have known where to begin looking. Neither Goode nor Gee is a rare name.

The following day, the results of the post mortem on Goode were available. Goode had not died from a combination of alcohol and antidepressant; it could not have been suicide. He had ingested, presumably in a glass of his whisky, an infusion or tincture–a few drops would be sufficient–made from the leaves or roots of *oenanthe crocata*, better known as horsebane or water lovage, a common plant which tastes sweet and not unpleasant but which is the most poisonous of British indigenous wild-flowers. If he had already been drinking, he might not have noticed the addition of the poison in his drink, and death from paralysis would have occurred within three hours.

Wickfield and Spooner were seated disconsolately in a pub in Tooting. The former was nursing a pint of bitter and a chicken sandwich, the latter a pint of Guinness and a house pie. They were in a discreet alcove shielded from eavesdroppers–if there had been any who wished to eavesdrop–and they were mulling over the latest developments in the case.

'We've got side-tracked, my lad, by all this F3P6 business. We can come back to them later to test their likelihood as assassins of Goode. We've forgotten an important point, so let's run over the sequence of events as we have tentatively reconstructed them. Goode comes to hear of a family estate in the wrong hands. He takes up genealogy, or perhaps his information came to him because he was already adept at the craft. He then joins an international organization which promises him help. After some time of gathering his information, perhaps years, he is ready to

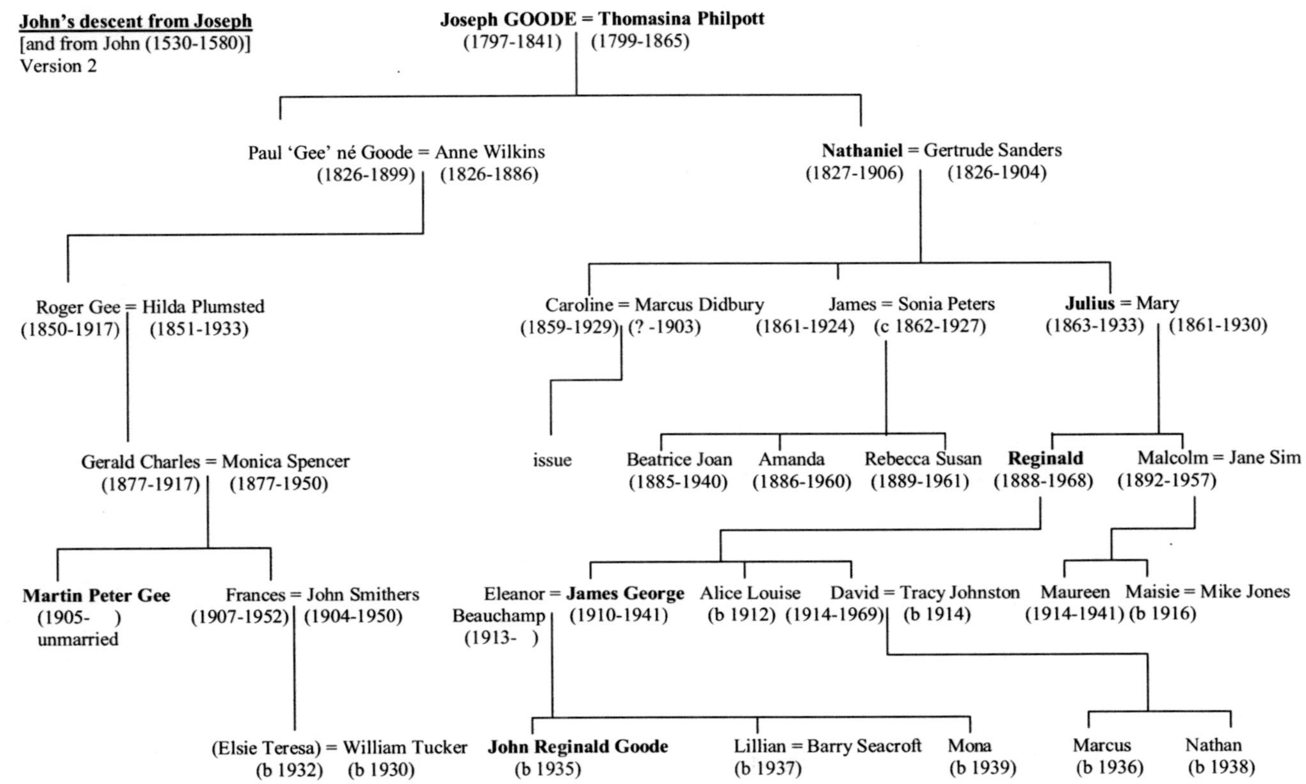

John's descent from Joseph
[and from John (1530-1580)]
Version 2
Joseph GOODE = **Thomasina Philpott**
(1797-1841) (1799-1865)
Paul 'Gee' né Goode = Anne Wilkins
(1826-1899) (1826-1886)
Nathaniel = Gertrude Sanders
(1827-1906) (1826-1904)
Roger Gee = Hilda Plumsted
(1850-1917) (1851-1933)
Caroline = Marcus Didbury
(1859-1929) (? -1903)
James = Sonia Peters
(1861-1924) (c 1862-1927)
Julius = Mary
(1863-1933) (1861-1930)
Gerald Charles = Monica Spencer
(1877-1917) (1877-1950)
issue
Beatrice Joan
(1885-1940)
Amanda
(1886-1960)
Rebecca Susan
(1889-1961)
Reginald
(1888-1968)
Malcolm = Jane Sim
(1892-1957)
Martin Peter Gee
(1905-)
unmarried
Frances = John Smithers
(1907-1952) (1904-1950)
Eleanor = **James George**
Beauchamp (1910-1941)
(1913-)
Alice Louise
(b 1912)
David = Tracy Johnston
(1914-1969) (b 1914)
Maureen
(1914-1941)
Maisie = Mike Jones
(b 1916)
(Elsie Teresa) = William Tucker
(b 1932) (b 1930)
John Reginald Goode
(b 1935)
Lillian = Barry Seacroft
(b 1937)
Mona
(b 1939)
Marcus
(b 1936)
Nathan
(b 1938)

launch his bid. There are two things he needs to do. First, he must eliminate an older Goode, namely Martin Gee. He might have risked getting away with it without that, but Gee's continuing existence would have remained a weak point in his position, if questions had been asked or his family trees challenged. With Gee out of the way, he, John Goode, was indisputably the senior male Goode alive and in the best position, genealogically speaking, to wrest the family estates from the Hotham usurper. Remember, we haven't yet proved or disproved Goode's claim: we're simply trying to work up a consistent framework to explain his actions, as we are reconstructing them.

'The second thing he needs to do is to put pressure on Hotham to yield the whole, or at least a large part, of the estates. He daren't let the matter go to court, for fear of jeopardizing his claim because of the Gee weak spot that we have identified, but he has possibly discovered something else which will enable him to tame Hotham, although that is speculation on my part. He is now ready, but a problem presents itself: how is he to get rid of Gee without leaving any trace of his own connection with the Gees? If he is suspected, the eliminated part of his family tree would be exposed and his own claim put at nought.

'He has traced Gee to a small village in the southern Midlands, where he is living in semi-retirement with years of life in him yet, all things being equal. It is not difficult to track down a named individual in Britain today, what with electoral rolls, telephone directories and so forth. All it needs is a bit of patience. He could have come across some of Gee's books or articles, and that would have made his search even easier. However, he now needs a plausible excuse to visit the village, remove his rival and disappear without leaving behind suspicion or trace. He decides to disguise himself as a stranger and gain entry to village life through a respected member of the community. But how? What he needs is an accomplice, someone known to him who, for a consideration, will put opportunity his way. Now it so happens–and here Providence is on his side–he knows someone living in Halton Thoresby. We'll return to that point shortly.

'This accomplice tips him off that certain villagers, the Matthewsons to be precise, are due to take a holiday in Cyprus at such and such a time, staying at such and such a hotel, the Mediterranean, or the Bella Vista, or the Hawaii Beach; included in the holiday is a two-day cruise to the Holy Land. Such exchange of information is commonplace in a village. Oh, where are you going on holiday? Cyprus? Lovely. When? Oh, do you want me to feed the cat for you? That sort of thing. It is now up to Goode to secure an introduction to this traveling couple, who have been described to him. He books in at the same hotel but avoids a confrontation until the cruise, to avoid suspicion of undue haste. Their meeting on the cruise appears to the Matthewsons to be entirely fortuitous, and they fall for the bait. They take to him sufficiently to invite him to their table on the boat and later to their house for Christmas. He parades as Thornton Dismore, something in banking, a young widower with a married niece: all perfectly above board, respectable and plausible.

'To add verisimilitude to his story, he rents a small flat in another part of London, under his assumed name–and this is perhaps where the F3P6 came in handy - puts down as much rent as he needs to avoid any embarrassing contretemps with the landlord, exchanges a few postcards or telephone-calls with the Matthewsons from his new, temporary flat, and his disguise is complete. The Matthewsons suspect nothing. Once he has obtained entry to their household for Christmas, he must perhaps play it by ear, looking for an opportunity to do away with Gee. He may have a number of ploys in mind. In the event, he chooses a heart drug, with the results we have witnessed, quietly ups sticks and disappears, on the pretext of urgent forgotten business before a lengthy trip abroad. Even if questions are asked, there can never be a connection made between Thornton Dismore of Summerskill Road, NW3 and John Goode of Tooting. He can then step forward as John Goode to claim his inheritance. Nobody knows of Gee as a Goode, but even if they did, his death could not be traced back to Goode.'

Spooner interrupted. 'Right, Sir,' he said, 'I follow you so far. All very ingenious. But why did Goode start to put pressure on Hotham in mid-December, before Gee was out of the way? He, Goode, still wasn't safe.'

'Good question,' replied Wickfield. 'You're certainly with me. I think that's why Goode gave Hotham a month to come up with a response. Goode was so excited and impatient, now that his plot was complete, that he couldn't wait until after Christmas to begin. He wanted to get the ball rolling and was confident of removing Gee in plenty of time. It is not difficult to murder someone when you are staying in the same village. He knows that to the Matthewsons and other Halton Thoresby villagers he is Thornton Dismore; to the Hothams in Rome he is John Goode. What likelihood was there that the Matthewsons and the Hothams would meet and compare notes? None at all. He is safe.'

'And the accomplice?' prompted Spooner.

'Ah, there's an interesting point. Look closely at the biographies you drew up while I was gallivanting about in Rome. Here they are.

Dr Wartenby **Simpson**, general practitioner. Mistletoe House, Cannington Road, Halton Thoresby. Born Manchester, 3 July 1920. Burrelton Grammar 1931-7, Birmingham University 1937-1943. General practice, Sutton Coldfield 1943-59, Cannington, 1959-73. Married Helen Worricker 1944. Children: David (b.1946), Carol (b.1948). Author of two papers: 'The Culture of the Abdomen' (1953) and 'Inflammatory Bowel Diseases' (1955).

Mrs Helen **Simpson**, librarian (retired). Mistletoe House, Cannington Road, Halton Thoresby. Née Worricker. Born Rugby, 4 September 1923. Chalfield Grammar 1935-41. MSc Information Studies Leeds University 1941-44. Assistant librarian, then librarian, Sutton Coldfield 1944-59, Cannington 1959-65. Married Dr Wartenby Simpson 1944. Children: as above. Interests: music (piano), literature, gardening. Active in WI and other local societies.

Mr Julius **Matthewson,** solicitor. Ashton House, The Green, Halton Thoresby. Born Bournemouth 12 October 1917. Bournemouth School for Boys 1929-35. Centre for Commercial

Law Studies, Exeter University 1935-42. Army service 1942-45. Junior then partner in firm of Bladud & Balding, Bolham, 1945-73. Married (1) Anne Plumtre 1936. Separated. (2) Deirdre Fisher 1946. No children. Interests: travel, philosophy, religion, walking.

Mrs Deirdre **Matthewson**, secretary (retired). Ashton House, The Green, Halton Thoresby. Born Yeovil 29 March 1918. The Poulton School, Yeovil 1929-34. Secretarial studies, Exeter Secretarial College 1934-36. School secretary Bolham 1936-51. Married Julius Matthewson 1946. No children. Interests: show-dogs, flower-arranging, bowls. Active in the church and WI.

Rev. Mr Simon **Thew**. The Vicarage, Halton Thoresby. Born London (Hammersmith) 1 June 1902. Morrison College 1913-19. Theology studies Sheffield University 1919-21, theological college (Hinton) 1921-24. Curate Shrewsbury (Mary the Virgin) 1924-29, Leicester (St Swithin's) 1929-37, vicar Didcot 1937-48, Halton Thoresby 1948-73. Married Rosemary Tubald 1933. Child: Peter (b.1937). Author of *Rogues of the Bible* (1930), *Wrestlers with Christ* (1935) and *Who's What in the Bible* (1939). Interests: reading, philately.

Mr George **Linford**, antique dealer. The Manor, Halton Thoresby. Born London (Chelsea) 15 January 1933. Beecham's School 1944-1951. Reading University (Fine Arts) 1951-54. Worked for Langham's of London as assessor in the furniture department 1954-67. Set up on his own in Birmingham 1967 to the present. Married Roberta Haldemann 1959. Interests: gardening, boating.

Mrs Roberta **Linford,** teacher. The Manor, Halton Thoresby. Née Haldemann.Born Nuneaton 18 November 1935. Mumford's School for Girls, Nuneaton 1946-51. University of Durham (Modern Languages) 1955-58. Teacher Cambridge Grammar School 1958-68, Curbridge Boys' College 1968-present. Interests: gardening, sailing, embroidery.

Mr Augustine **Vickers**, company director. Anchor Lodge, Holly Lane, Halton Thoresby. Born Tewksbury 4 August 1929. Tewksbury High School 1941-47. Grimsby Polytechnic 1947-50. Various jobs in lower management, ending up as retail manager for Gordon Compressors (Worcester) Ltd. Company director 1969-1973. Married Sarah Jope 1957. Children: Benedict (b.1958), Brian (b.1959). Interests: walking, French history, professional football.

Mrs Sally **Vickers**, nurse. Anchor Lodge, Holly Lane, Halton Thoresby. Born Carlisle 10 September 1928. Secondary schooling in Kenya. Nursing college in London 1946-49. St Dorothy's Hospital for the Infirm, Hastings, 1949-51, Huddleston Hospital, Worcester 1951-65, Worcester General Hospital 1965-1973. Married 1957. Children as above. Interests: literature, music (cello, piano), the countryside.

'There can be no doubt, on the basis of all this information, which one is Goode's accomplice. Now, we have already seen the function this accomplice fulfilled: to inform Goode of a way of ingratiating himself with a couple of the villagers. For what reward? Probably a share in the winnings, a cash sum, but I am only speculating. It could have been to repay a past favor, or to satisfy some personal grudge against Gee, and we have seen that enough villagers satisfy that requirement.

'Let us speculate further. What if the relationship between Gee and his accomplice turns sour? There could be a number of reasons for this we have no idea about at the moment. Perhaps Goode refuses to cough up, or cough up as much as he'd promised. Or perhaps he has information which he could use against the accomplice. The latter travels to London, murders Goode and returns to Halton Thoresby. No reward, certainly, but no danger of exposure as a party to the scam either. Or perhaps–and here I am straying quite a bit from my script–perhaps the accomplice is in a position to make a personal bid for the Goode estates by using the same lever on Hotham as Goode had used. We don't know how much of Joan Goode's will or his plot to benefit from it he had disclosed.'

'So who do you think this accomplice is?' asked Spooner. 'I'm certain I can't come up with an answer. Half the villagers look plausible to me, with the possible exception of the vicar's wife!'

'Well, I may be proved wrong, and this goes no further than the two of us, but my guess is Mrs Roberta Linford.'

'How on earth do you figure that out? There's nothing in these biographies that even suggests it!'

'Oh, but there is. Think of it this way. Apart from the personal interests of the individuals named, the biographies give you two dimensions, history and geography. We've been given no reason yet to suppose that Goode had only lately come to know any of the Halton Thoresby villagers; their acquaintance was therefore long-standing. I'm thinking aloud, you understand. Now few people keep up with friends from primary school–so few that I think for our present purposes we can discount it. Most people retain one or perhaps two friends at most from secondary school–I'm talking about still being friends ten, twenty years later. Now John Goode could not have shared a secondary school with any of the people on our list. If you look at the biographies, never have John Goode and any of our suspects been in the same place for purposes of family life, schooling or work. But there is one place where they could have coincided: university! Your choice of university at the age of eighteen has nothing usually to do with geography but all to do with the courses you wish to follow and your future career ambitions. You find that university students come from all over the place, because they are prepared to travel to get what they want–or where they can get in. Now only one of our candidates matches Goode in age, namely Mrs Linford. If she and Goode were at Durham together, they would have been there at exactly the same time. Furthermore, while we know that she read Modern Languages, Goode also had an interest in languages, which we can deduce because of the French books on his book-shelves. I shall therefore wager you a tin of sardines to a tub of sour cream that John Goode read Modern Languages at Durham before bailing out, and that it was there he met the gracious Mrs Linford, or Miss Haldemann as she would have been then. Fifteen or sixteen years have passed since their university days together, but they could well have kept up with each other, in however a desultory way.'

'Not bad, Sir, but all a bit vague.'

'Oh, I grant you that, but the precise identification of our accomplice is not vital at this stage. If only we could to set a trap to encourage the party to betray his or her identity. The culprit would then be held on suspicion of the murder of John Goode and of being an accessory to the murder to Martin Gee.'

'And if you don't mind my asking, Sir, what form would this flushing-out take?'

'Ah, there we should have to be quite subtle. The way I see it is this. The minute Goode has obtained Hotham's acquiescence to his scheme–that's in the course of their conversation in London on 28 December–he phones his accomplice in Halton Thoresby–let us call her Mrs X–to call off the deal between the two of them, whatever it was. If Mrs X kicks up a fuss, he simply threatens to implicate her in his downfall. She travels post haste up to London, confronts him with his treachery and kills him. She dresses his death up to look like suicide, hastens back to Halton Thoresby and awaits developments, if any.

'If this reconstruction is in any way close to the mark, there are three things that Mrs X does not know:

1. whether Goode's death is regarded by the police as suicide or murder or possibly accidental overdose. She must be very naïve if she thinks the pathologist is going to miss a draught of horsebane, but one never knows;
2. whether the police have made the connection between Thornton Dismore and Goode;
3. most importantly, whether Hotham has actually agreed to hand over three-quarters of his estate to John Goode.

On the other hand, she, or possibly he, knows three things that can be known only by Goode's murderer–if we restrict our circle of suspects to villagers of Halton Thoresby, that is:

1. that Goode and Dismore are the same person;
2. that, as a Goode, Gee is an obstacle to Goode's ambitions;
3. that Goode murdered Gee.

I wonder … '

I leave my character behind me.

.Richard Sheridan, School for Scandal Act II, scene 2.

Reluctant himself to face the task of telling Mrs Goode, a woman of sixty, whom he had never before met and about whom he knew virtually nothing, firstly that her eldest child and only son had been found dead in his flat, but secondly, that he had been the victim of a murder at the age of thirty-eight, Detective Inspector Wickfield was happy to observe the conventions of police protocol and invite a WPC at the local station to bear the crushing news and then to sit with the lady while she composed herself. Wickfield turned up several hours later. Spooner meanwhile was deputed to interview anyone from F3P6 he could get hold of.

'Mrs Goode,' he began, 'I am so sorry to have to trouble you at this moment, but in a murder case, time is important. I want you, if you will, to talk to me about your son, so that I can build up a clearer picture of him in my mind. I never met him, remember.'

Mrs Goode, her handkerchief to her mouth, looked at him full of trouble and grief. She said nothing but nodded in understanding and acquiescence.

'Thank you, WPC Grant, you may return to the station now, if you wish. I shall make Mrs Goode another cup of tea, and we shall chat for a while about John.'

The inspector knew that after bereavement, when that bereavement is unexpected and one has not, for example, been at a hospital bedside for weeks on end or watching a slow decline spread out over months or years, the mental functions close down to some extent with the purpose of numbing the blow. He took his time.

'Mrs Goode, thank you for being so understanding. Could you tell me a little bit about John as a child?'

'Yes, of course. I won't pretend he was an easy child - I'm sorry, I've forgotten your rank and name already!'

'It's Wickfield, Detective Inspector.'

'Inspector, then. Oh, it's so difficult to understand that he has gone from us!'

After a few quiet sobs, she resumed.

'John wasn't an easy child. He could be moody and solitary, but he was dear to us. He never got over his father's death, you know. James was called up in 1940, and the following year he was killed in France. John, of course, was too young to know what was happening, but as he saw things, his father left us just as times were becoming difficult, and never came back. James left us poor. I had three young children and no savings, and life was a struggle. I earned a living by taking in washing, helping out in the corner shop, charring–anything I could get hold of. We had no luxuries in the house. Fortunately my sister Jane helped out with feeding the girls, shopping–when there was anything in the shops–and household chores, otherwise I'd never have managed.

'I remember once John coming home from school, all of five years old. This was just after James had gone off to the war. He was in tears because the teacher had told him off and he didn't see why. He'd identified an ﬂ sign in a printed book as a capital A, and he couldn't understand the difference even when it was pointed out to him. I think that was the start of deep feelings of inadequacy. Another incident I remember was a few years later: John was eleven or twelve, I suppose. I had the three children, and my sister and her husband had joined us for a picnic in the country. We came to a stream, little more than a trickle really, and we all went to cross by the bridge. John shouted to us that he would use boulders as stepping-stones and that we lacked any sense of adventure. I told him he'd fall in and that he would do much better to come with us. No, he wouldn't have it: he jumped on to a boulder, slipped, and fell into the stream up to his ankles. We all laughed, but I could see that he again thought of himself as a failure.'

'How did John do at school, Mrs Goode?'

'Not bad. Not brilliant, but he kept up with the rest. He got a place at grammar school, you see. We lived in Ipswich then, where John was born and his father before him. He couldn't get on with the sciences, not very well, anyway, although he was good at maths, but he loved history and English, and I think he got a bit of a crush on the geography teacher, because he went on from O-Level geography to A-level when he really wasn't good enough. In the end he settled for modern languages at university.'

'Which university did he go to, Mrs Goode?'

'Durham. He was offered a place at Exeter, but a friend of his at school was going to Durham, so John decided to go there as well.'

'How did he get on?'

'He didn't. Left after a year. Something to do with a girl. Puppy love to you and me, but he took it very seriously, and when she ditched him, his world fell apart. He never really recovered from this.'

More sobs. The inspector was happy to let the grief take its course. He was building up a picture of this lad, to some extent the victim of circumstances, to some extent the victim of his own defects. He was not in a hurry.

'He couldn't face the thought of another girl-friend after that. Too afraid of getting rebuffed. When he came down from Durham that summer, he was in a bad way. Said he was a failure. Couldn't manage to study, couldn't keep a girl-friend, no career prospects, no money etc. "What does life hold for the likes of me?" he'd say. "I'm not worth the space I occupy." What could I say to these outpourings of inadequacy? I assured him again and again of my love for him, but he said that wasn't enough.'

'What about his sisters? Were they any help?'

'They did their best, poor dears, but they were younger and even more helpless than I was. Lil was seventeen, Mona fifteen, both still at school, with their own problems of study, boy-friends, spots, hair and all the other problems teenagers give themselves.'

'Did they normally get on with John?'

'Oh, yes, but of course their girl-friends were no help, because they were all too young for him. So his self-esteem never recovered. Or that's how it appears to me.'

'So what did John do then, Mrs Goode?'

'He drifted. Moved to London, got a series of small jobs, didn't settle at anything. He'd come home every few months hoping for a handout–and of course I gave him what I could, but money was tight. I could see him turning in on himself–even more than before–and I felt helpless. If I'd had more money, I could have done more. Then suddenly his luck turned, in the sense that he got a small job in a bank as a teller. It suited him, you see. No responsibility, just follow procedures, no one to impress. Because he could manage the work, he regained some of his self-esteem, but he was aware all the time that the job was humble, that it didn't pay well, that his prospects were not dazzling, and so on.'

'Mrs Goode, how did John get into genealogy, do you know?'

'Yes, I do, funnily enough, because he told me all about it one day when he was visiting me here in Ipswich not long after he'd moved to London. He was out of work at the time, or working only part-time, I forget which, and one morning he wandered in to a public library to get warm. On one of the reading-desks somebody had left an introduction to genealogy called something like *Get to Know Your Ancestors*, and the frontispiece was a coat of arms in full color, with all the scrolls and squiggles and a motto in Latin and goodness knows what heraldic beasts rampant and couchant, or whatever the terms are, and John was hooked. He joined the library there and then in order to be able to take this particular book away with him. It didn't take him long to work through it–it was only an introduction, after all–and very soon he was reading heftier volumes with titles like *Genealogy for the Serious Researcher* and *Practical Aids to Advanced Genealogy.* He began to save his money to buy books that he could read at his leisure and mark or comment on in the margin. Part of this was, of course, a study of his own family. I couldn't help him very much, because I hadn't a clue about even my husband's grandparents, both of whom were dead before I met James, let alone his great-grandparents, but he got a bit of help from his aunt Alice, and that was it: he was off!'

'Did he make any startling discoveries–that he was descended from William the Conqueror, for example?'

'Oh, no. He explained to me that only very few families could go back with certainty beyond 1532, but he also said that connecting yourself with prominent historical figures was not the point. Genealogy gave you pride in the achievements of your own family, however modest, and that was what mattered. If your family showed any signs of improving their lot and that of society, all the better: you could be part of that.'

'Do you know how far back John got?'

'No, after a time he became a little secretive about his researches, or perhaps a better word would be reticent. He would say that his part of the Goode family had never really distinguished itself, and he wouldn't bore me with petty details of mistresses and illegitimacy and humble jobs, but I guessed that the subject was constantly on his mind. On the few occasions I went up to London to see him, his tables were always covered with papers and documents to do with family history. He did say at one point that the family had once achieved a respectable status in society but that it had all been lost through an unfortunate death, but I don't know any details. Why do you ask?'

'Mrs Goode, I will be frank with you, and what I am about to say may come as a bit of a shock to you. I am very uncertain in my facts, so I beg you to understand that I am making no accusations.'

He paused to let his words sink in. This poor lady had enough to occupy her mind at the moment, but he had to raise this matter with her to be surer of his ground.

'There is some reason to believe that John discovered the existence of a remote cousin who stood between him and a considerable family fortune. At Christmas-time, he took the opportunity of looking up this cousin, and there is a faint suggestion that he brought about his death in order to benefit from the opportunity of an inheritance. Do you think that John would have been capable of murder?'

He could see that his words had shocked John's mother. She was struggling to come to terms with this latest extraordinary intelligence. Murder? Good Heavens, please don't say so!

After a while, she spoke, calmly enough.

'Inspector, I will try to be honest with you. John had many faults–all of us do, I daresay. He had become obsessed with his family researches. I suspected that he found in his ancestors a sense of achievement that he couldn't derive from his own life. He got on with his ancestors! They couldn't correct him or look down on him. They gave him a sense of belonging. He had lost his father but gained umpteen grandfathers! John was introverted, perhaps one would call him selfish, or at least self-centered, and I think there was a certain ruthlessness in his make-up as a foil to his sense of failure: if people don't take to me voluntarily, I'll impose myself! But really, Inspector, I'm not a psychologist, I'm only thinking aloud. I should hate to think my son capable of murder. He might be tempted to trample on other people, but surely not to the extent of murder! No, I really don't think so.'

'Thank you, Mrs Goode, you have been very helpful. I'm so sorry to have to raise these matters with you. There is one other thing, and I hope you will forgive me for bringing it up. Your John apparently belonged to a somewhat mysterious organization called F3P6. Can you tell me what you know about that?'

'Sorry, Inspector, I've no idea what you're talking about. That's the first I've ever heard of it. You could try John's sister Lil: he used to confide in her quite a bit, I think.'

'And her address, Mrs Goode?'

The inspector's visit to Mrs Lillian Seacroft proved valuable only in the sense that it gave him a feel for the wider Goode family, since present on the occasion of his visit were Lil's husband Barry and her cousin Marcus. The Seacroft residence was in Fountains Road, not far from Bourne Park, a 1930s semi-detached house that betrayed the family's middle-class status perhaps more clearly than clothes, accent or employment could have done. Wickfield was decently if not warmly received and felt that they were willing, if not precisely keen, despite protestations to the contrary, to cooperate.

'Mrs Seacroft, I hope you will forgive this intrusion on you at a time of family grief, but I'm looking for answers to some questions, and your mother said you might be able to help.'

'Yes, Inspector, she phoned to say you might be calling. We'll help in any way we can, of course. By the way, this is my husband, Barry, and my cousin Marcus.'

'Pleased to meet you, Gentlemen. I shall be brief, Mrs Seacroft, because I don't want to take up your time. Your brother John belonged to an organization called F3P6. Do you know how long he'd been a member?'

Marcus interrupted. 'Just like cousin John to go for the weird and wonderful! Why couldn't he belong to something sensible like the National Trust?'

'Perhaps he did, Sir, but all we're interested in at the moment is F3P6.'

'What is the organization for, Inspector?' asked Mrs Seacroft.

'It helps people wishing to research their family history and restore family fortunes.'

'Oh, well, that would be just up John's street, because he was potty about the Goodes. Had quite a bee in his bonnet about a Joan Goode, I remember, who'd been diddled out of a lot of money–or perhaps she'd diddled somebody else out of a lot of money. John said that the money should be ours by rights. I never took him seriously.'

'You shouldn't either, Inspector,' said Marcus. 'John's fiddling about with his books and now his membership of a mysterious organization, which is news to us, got him nowhere, I can assure you. If he'd discovered a treasure in deepest Yorkshire, he would have told us about it.'

Would he, though? thought the inspector. I doubt it. He seemingly did not even tell his own mother.

John's sister Mona was apparently away in America somewhere, working at a holiday camp, but the inspector thought that a visit to Aunt Alice might be productive. Aunt Alice lived in a terraced house in Ipswich, not far from her sister-in-law's. Where Eleanor was a stout woman with hard work under her finger-nails and rough features softened by personal warmth, Alice was well groomed and (thought Wickfield) not familiar with exertion. She greeted him politely enough but opined that she was unlikely to be of any help as she had never really got on with John: Marcus and Nathan, her other brother's children, yes, they were straightforward boys, plenty of life, fun to be with, but John had always been a bit shy or inward-looking, even secretive.

'Miss Goode, we're trying to find out how deeply involved John was with a genealogical organization called F3P6. Do you know anything about his membership of it?'

'It's funny you should ask that, but it so happens I do know something about it. It was like this. Some years ago now, John came to see me, not because we are close but because I had not long before come into a respectable win on the pools. He wanted a loan to help with a bit of research, so he said. I was not going to part with money on a whim, so I questioned him more closely. He didn't exactly swear me to secrecy, but he made it plain that he was telling me reluctantly and would much rather it went no further. Well, to be honest, Inspector, it was all of so little interest to me that I wouldn't have bothered telling anyone else anyway. In the course of his researches in London, he'd come across a will of 1700-and-something which he took very seriously. It showed, he told me quite excitedly, that a large estate in Yorkshire, which ended up in the hands of some unworthy ruffian, should by rights have come to us. It all seemed so far-fetched that I took very little notice of the details as he poured out the story. The long and the short of it was that the background to this amazing will had to be researched in Yorkshire. He had a fortnight's holiday coming up, wanted to spend the time in the Borthwick, County Library, County Records Office and goodness knows where else, but had no money at all for travel or accommodation. Could I help?'

'Just a minute, Miss Goode. Can you remember when this was?'

'Let me see. I had my pools win in January of 1968. It must have been about four months later that John came to see me. Is it important, Inspector?'

'No, probably not. But please go on.'

'Well, I said, I'll help, but I wonder whether you wouldn't be better to go to F3P6, who sound as if they can put a lot more resources at your disposal than I can.'

'How on earth had you come to hear of F3P6?'

'Through the library. I had not long borrowed a lovely romance–*The Rose-Red Damsel*, it was called: ooh, a smashing story, I loved it–read it twice right through–and inside it was a flier for this organization. I thought the library had perhaps left it in all their books that day as a sort of advertisement. So I gave John the flier: I'd just put it on the mantle-piece, because on the front of it was a pretty coat of arms. John read it through, seemed to get quite excited about it; thought it might be just what he was looking for; and went!'

'Did John ever tell you whether he applied to join F3P6?'

'No, he didn't, but I didn't really expect to hear from him: we didn't correspond or meet with any regularity, you understand. In any event, he never came back to me about the loan, so I presume he got fixed up somehow.'

'Thank, Miss Goode, that's all very helpful. Does the name Hotham mean anything to you?'

'No, I don't think so. Wait a minute, though, wasn't that the promiscuous bloke John said had got all our money? Or was that Holtham? Or Witham? No, sorry, it's gone. Take no notice of me. No, I don't know the name Hotham!'

'Miss Goode, you have been very generous with your time. I only wish all the people we dealt with were as helpful!'

XIV

The very marrow of tradition's shown.
Charles Lamb, To the Editor of the Every-Day Book

Detective Sergeant Spooner realized that the task delegated to him by his superior was not an easy one. It is possible, so ran the temporary hypothesis, that F3P6 had a hand in John Goode's death. If no illegality had been perpetrated in Goode's bid to recover the lost fortune, secrecy was unwarranted; but if F3P6 had either condoned or even committed an act of murder in the furtherance of Goode's aims, it had every reason to conceal its operation. The management would necessarily deny all connection with Goode, except to admit his membership, registration paid, advice received, nothing more. How to lead them to the point of admitting that legal boundaries had been transgressed, that was the problem.

Following the postal contact details given on the flier, Spooner was eventually put in touch with a Mr John Smith, and the two men met in a café behind the British Museum–it doesn't come much more cloak-and-dagger than that, thought Spooner. Mr Smith was a tall, gaunt gentleman in his early seventies (he judged). Sparse grey hair nearly covered a high dome of cranium. Rimless spectacles sat on the top of his nose. Keen blue eyes looked out over sunken cheeks. Long, lean fingers reminded Spooner of a spider. Mr Smith was immaculately dressed in a bespoke suit of navy blue, with matching waistcoat, and a red patterned tie that relieved the plainness of the sky-blue shirt. He was every inch an aristocrat.

'Mr Smith. Pardon my impertinence, Sir, but I presume that is not your real name?'

'No, Sergeant, there's no deceiving the British police, is there? I am Graf Gaspar Otto Johannes von Staβbaum von und zu Meβenhaupt, but my friends call me Otto. Please feel free to do likewise.'

'Thank you for agreeing to meet me, Count Otto'–he would meet him half-way. 'You speak excellent English, if I may say so.'

'My governess was English–but thank you, anyway.'

'As I told you in my note, I am here on behalf of the Worcestershire CID in connection with the recent death of John Goode. We understand that Mr Goode was a member of your organization.'

'Yes, that is, he registered with us some years ago–I have the details here if you wish them–and was in regular touch, until last year, as his researches continued and expanded.'

'Can you tell me what assistance you were able to render him?'

'Normally, of course, Sergeant, you will appreciate that we cannot discuss individual members or their business, but I am prepared to divulge details of John Goode's case, as you are engaged in a murder investigation. And he is dead, of course.'

Here Mr Smith consulted his dossier. Spooner noticed that on the front of the dossier was simply a reference number: no name or other identifying feature.

'Mr Goode came to consult us five years ago, or thereabouts. His problem was purely financial. He outlined his needs to us and we proceeded on that basis. We required some proof, of course, of his story. He produced a facsimile of an eighteenth-century will in which an estate was bequeathed with a condition attached. He proceeded to show that the family who were granted the estate did not seem to have fulfilled the condition, and he showed us also, somewhat sketchily, that his own family had a prior claim. What he needed to do was to dot all the i's and cross all the t's. For that he needed funds. We were so far convinced of the essential legitimacy of his case that we undertook to advance a sum of money as a gift, with more to come provided that he could show us the fruits of his labors.'

Here Mr Smith consulted his dossier again.

'He returned to us a year later. He had produced a convincing family tree–as far as it went–and information that a cemetery in Bologna provided additional proof that the receiving family had betrayed their trust. We were happy to subsidize him further.

'A year later he returned, this time with three bulky files detailing three family histories: the Goodes, leading up to the testatrix Joan; a junior branch of the family leading up to himself; and the Hothams of (supposedly) Kellythwaite and Rome. Our in-house genealogists spent a year checking over the files and were eventually satisfied as to the legitimacy of Mr Goode's claim.'

Here he paused.

Spooner interjected: 'There was a problem?'

'Well, Sergeant, I will be quite frank with you. We could not recommend that Mr Goode took his claim to court, despite the wealth of information he had provided.'

'Why was that?'

Mr Smith produced part of the family tree with which Spooner was familiar–the sanitized version.

'You see, Sergeant, there was a male Goode born, one Paul, whose family might have had a prior claim to John Goode's if it had survived. The tree showed that he was born in 1826, with the added noted 'died in infancy'. Now if this child had *not* died in infancy, John Goode's genealogical position might be quite different. Goode professed that he had not been able to uncover any further information about this child, despite extensive researches, and that it was a reasonable contention, that would persuade any unbiassed court, that the boy had not survived infancy. Our experts did not quite agree with him on that, and the association of F3P6 and Mr Goode came to an end last year, a shade acidly on his part, I have to admit. We were sorry not to be able to carry his project through to its term, as its aims accorded precisely with the aims of our founder.'

'Ah,' said Spooner, 'I should like to come to those in a minute, but could you tell me first what you know about Mr Goode's plan? Did he implement it after he had left you, do you know?'

'Can't help you there at all, Sergeant, or at least not much. In my last conversation with Mr Goode'–he rummaged through the dossier–'on 7 December 1973, he said he thought he saw the possibility of negotiating with the present incumbent. Of course, we regarded that as a private matter between him and Mr Hotham and were not prepared to intervene or to lean on anybody or to take part in any kind of threat–not our style at all, Sergeant–so, as I say, we parted company. On the other hand, I did leave the door open, offering our continued services to Mr Goode should he see his way to adopting another course of action. I am therefore a little out of touch, you see.'

'Count Otto, you are being very helpful, and believe me, I appreciate your assistance. We come now to a rather delicate matter which I am quite sure will go no further than this cup of tea.'

He paused for the Count's agreement.

'Sergeant, you can rely entirely on my discretion.'

'Thank you, Otto. We have reason to believe that John Goode did, as you surmised he might, run across a prior heir to the Goode estate, a distant cousin who went by the name of Martin Gee.' Here he brought out of his brief-case the unbowdlerized version of the part of the tree the Count had just shown him. The Count took a few minutes to study it.

'Ah!' he said.

'Now we believe–and I stress that this is only supposition, so I am not making any accusations–that John Goode schemed to do away with Martin Gee in order then to claim the estate for himself by blackmailing Mr Hotham into yielding to his pressure. It is also a supposition on our part that F3P6 gave him added assistance in the murder of Martin Gee. A certain Mr Thornton Dismore–which is almost certainly a pseudonym derived from Joan Goode's will and family tree–figures in this case as a possible assassin. Could he, Count Otto, have conceivably been one of your operatives?'

'No, Sergeant, a thousand times no. That is not at all the way we operate.'

'Could he have been a maverick operative of yours, acting on his own initiative encouraged, perhaps, by an inducement from our deceased friend Mr Goode?'

'No, quite impossible. You see, Mr Goode met no member of the Foundation apart from me. I was able to refer his case directly to the Board in Switzerland and to submit his work to our in-house specialists here without his needing to meet them. In short, I was always the only member of F3P6 management that Goode met. He had access to no one else.'

'But wasn't his dossier open to inspection by other members of the Foundation who could have contacted him without your knowledge?'

'I can assure you, Sergeant, that none of our other members would act independently of the Foundation, even if they had been aware of Goode's intentions, which I doubt. You see, all contact details are kept separately from the dossiers, and only I have access to them in the UK. Our other branches have a similar system. The members of the Board are above suspicion.'

'Thank you, that all seems perfectly clear. Now you said earlier that John Goode's case was just up your street, or words to that effect. Could you clarify that for me?'

'Yes, willingly. Our founder, François Peyerolle de Montmorillon, was a man of vision. He was dismayed by the havoc wrought by two world wars, in one area in particular: the European patrimony, the magnificent heritage of generations of European families who had been responsible for making Europe what it is–or was before 1939. Not just war, of course: the rise of communism and the expansion of the Soviet empire had deprived scores of notable families of their latifundial base; Nazism likewise. There had been religious persecutions. All in all, Europe's greatest families had been squeezed and buffeted and sadly reduced. Peyerolle was one of the lucky ones: his Swiss empire had remained intact. He determined to use his money to help those less fortunate than himself.

'Now you must realize that his aims were not élitist. He purposed to benefit the *polloi*–I use that word without any disparagement intended–the *many*, shall we say, by ensuring the survival or reinstatement of the social framework which made the progress of *all* possible. By that he meant the political, financial, agrarian, urban and rural structures which supported the work of leading families. You will appreciate at once that this laudable aim had a historical dimension. Not every one who jumped up and said, Yes, I can lead Europe, was to be believed. The families Peyerolle wished to support had to have a proved track-record in terms of latifundial management, social leadership, breadth of social vision, sense of heritage and so on. If their property was being well conducted and exploited to the benefit of the many, even if it was in the wrong hands, he was reluctant to intervene. His delight was to *restore* to rightful owners property or wealth that was being mismanaged by usurpers.

'Let me give you a classic example: myself. My family had an estate in Germany that was the envy of thousands. In the middle of it was set a magnificent fifteenth-century *Schloß*, and from here my forebears managed parkland, woodland, farms, villages, a variety of enterprises and rural trades for the benefit of their tenants. The Nazis confiscated the entire property, and under their gentle care the castle burnt down in 1942. The lands had already been apportioned to Nazi apparatchiks, but they cared little for the proper management of them. At the end of the war, the pretended owners had disappeared, the land was lying fallow, the former tenants, having no landlord and so no work, drifted to the towns. When I and my wife returned to view our ancestral lands in 1948, the prospect of restoration seemed hopeless.

'A year later we heard of F3P6 and registered. It was Peyerolle himself who dealt with our case. We had traveled to Switzerland, to his château on Lake Geneva, and were warmly received. He enabled us to supplement our savings in order to buy the ruined property back; he guided us, through his team of hired experts, in the huge enterprise of encouraging tenants to re-invest their time, skills and indeed lives in the estate, of reclaiming arable land, managing decayed woods, promoting local trades and markets. Our tenants and ourselves, with our sons, then worked hard to restore the *Schloß* to its former magnificence.'

Here the count reached into his wallet and withdrew a photo of an elaborate castle, complete with moat, pepper-pot towers, turrets and machicolations, all in splendid order.

'We owe everything to François,' he continued, 'and the excellently managed estate you now see at Staßbaum is really his creation. I have retired from active management of it, but my sons and their wives continue the centuries-old family traditions of capable husbandry, service to the local communities and the highest moral standards befitting hereditary gentlemen.

'Let me give you another example, a simpler one. A certain Polish aristocrat came to us a year or so ago–let us call him the Markiz Rawicz, although I don't actually know either his title or his surname. The family were apparently beyond reproach: ancient–the present marquis (if marquis he was, or grand duke, or baron, it doesn't matter) was the fourteenth of that title–wealthy, stable, model aristocratic citizens in a part of Poland not overrun with good aristocrats. His problem was that he had no sons to carry on either the title or the name. He could have invested them in his daughter, but he was unwilling to do so for fear that, in any divorce, for example, the whole or part of the heritage should pass out of Rawicz hands. How could he get a male heir who would satisfy the requirements of genetic legitimacy and historical awareness? Our genealogists were able to locate a Rawicz of whom he was unaware–the great-great-nephew of a great-uncle - and we were then able to advise him on the legal aspects of adoption, inheritance and so forth which would guarantee the continuance of the estate, as a unit, into the next generation without legal problems. He could have done all this himself, I suppose, at a pinch, but he relied on our expertise and experience to simplify matters and ensure the smooth fulfillment of his wishes. In any case, we were able to conduct his case in much less time than he would have required if he had been working with his own resources only.

'Now when Mr Goode came to see me, and as his case matured, I came to realize that an injustice had been indeed been done. I looked carefully at the Yorkshire estates. I came to the conclusion that the traditional family home, Kellythwaite Park, was probably not recoverable, unless by some chance it came on the open market, but the estate was another proposition. The present owners, however well-meaning, live abroad, care only half-heartedly for the patrimony and have allowed the estate to stagnate. It is merely ticking over. I was not convinced that John Goode was precisely the right person to restore its fortunes, but, with guidance from the Foundation, I thought he was sufficiently focussed to take it on. Also, he fell comfortably into the 30-44 age-range, which many sociologists consider the most innovative and active. In any case, his financial requirements from us were trifling compared with some, so our investment in him was not a heavy one. There was one other consideration that weighed heavily with me, in line with the thinking of our blessed Founder as expounded in his work *Progrés en Europe et la Contribution de certaines Familles Importantes*, of which you may know. John Goode had in his bones, in his very marrow, the genes of the ancient family. It is true that nothing much came of them for a time, but I gather that that was due to a combination of lack of opportunity and unfortunate circumstances–unless Goode was, as you English say, spinning me a line. His claim to Goode genes is in any case better founded than that of Mr Hotham.'

The Count suddenly switched tack.

'Are you a married man, Sergeant?'

'Yes, and I have a small daughter–very small, as yet.'

'Then you will appreciate, at least to some extent, the pride that fires a man in the presence of his family. When you add in that that family exists and prospers for perhaps six or seven hundred years, you can begin to appreciate the pride people can take in their ancestry: the same house, perhaps, the same lands, recurrent family names, a history, a tradition. That is what we are here for, Sergeant: to preserve that tradition.'

'Can I ask a question? If it's a silly one, I'm sure you'll tell me so. Don't families have what you might call a "natural life"? Like states and empires, they rise, prosper and fall, don't they? Aren't you therefore interfering with what seems to be a law of nature?'

'No, my friend, that is a very good question, and it is one to which our Founder devotes an entire chapter in his book. Yes, of course, families rise and fall. For example, the Medicis are no longer with us: you may have read Hibbert's recent study on *The Rise* and Fall *of the House of Medici*. Not to mention that literature is riddled with the collapse or decline of famous houses: Usher, Avenel, Forsyte, Lampedusa and so on. Our point is, how can you determine the "natural life" of a family? States decay because they collapse from within; similarly families. Peyerolle identifies the signals to look for. We intervene, however, when a family is in trouble not from inner decay but from external circumstances with which at that moment the family is powerless to grapple.'

Both remained silent for a while.

'I wonder whether you can explain something else for me,' began Sergeant Spooner, producing from his brief-case the document they had found in Gee's flat: 'The new member of F3P6' etc. 'This document seems to contradict what you were saying earlier, Count Otto. Why did you not tell me about it?'

'Sergeant, I know of this unfortunate document, but I can assure you that it has nothing to do with us at all. Let me explain. A few years ago we were infiltrated by two members of a right-wing group sympathetic to the aims of the Nazi party. They managed over a period of time to get themselves elected to the Board, and they began to produce this document in our name as a vehicle for their own disgraceful philosophy. It took us some time to realize the reality of the situation, and we took immediate action. Since then, our procedures have been considerably tightened, and I do not think there can be a recurrence. So you see, Sergeant, there is nothing mysterious or sinister about F3P6, as you might infer from this distasteful literature. We are discreet, we are confidential, we work out of the public gaze. We are a charitable organization, not a front for subversive activities.'

'How do you think Goode got hold of this pernicious leaflet? Could our friend Mr Dismore have had a hand in it?'

'Sergeant, you know more of Mr Dismore than I do. Once a document exists, it lurks. I daresay if you went to certain libraries and consulted copies of Peyerolle's work, you would find examples of this leaflet tucked inside. That is what I imagine may have happened. But I can assure you, with absolute confidence, that Goode never received this or any similar document from us.'

'Could this neo-Nazi wing or cell, which you tell me was expelled as soon as you got wind of it, still be operating? Could John Goode have got in touch with it? I'm only thinking that if he was involved with it and somehow, in the words of the leaflet, "betrayed it", they could have decided to punish him.'

'Sergeant, I really have no idea. We have not been troubled by these people since they were expelled, and I have no idea what happened to them. They were and are of no interest to us whatever. Please hold us entirely guiltless of anything that has happened to Mr Goode.'

The two parted. Sergeant Spooner was convinced that F3P6 was irrelevant to their inquiry.

XV

Touch us gently, Time!
Let us glide adown thy stream
Gently, - as we sometimes glide
Through a quiet dream.

Bryan W.Procter (1787-1874), Touch us gently, Time

It may not be impossible for us
to shape out some little supplementary conspiracy of our own.

Sir Walter Scott, The Black Dwarf, Chapter IV

The inspector's imagination took wings. In the national newspaper read by our suspect - he mused - which had been ascertained by Constable Pudden (although the constable was adamant that no member of that set would dream of buying any daily national except the *Daily Observer*, so it had hardly been worth his while to inquire), a false notification concerning Goode's murder would be inserted. At the same time, a paragraph would be inserted into the *Cannington Herald* stating that the police, now quite satisfied that Gee's death was an accident, had closed the case. These two newspaper insertions were to satisfy Mrs X that all danger is past. She could safely acknowledge a connection with both Gee–that went without saying–and Goode, the alleged murderer of Gee. The bait was to be a share in the Goode estate as if it had gone to Gee. If the identity of Dismore and Goode transpired, she would concoct some pretext about being unaware of anything illegal in Goode's maneuvers. For this trap to be plausible, the police would have to allow for failure if Mrs X came up with a good enough story.

He pursued this line of thought and in his mind's eye framed the notices as follows in, respectively, the *Daily Observer* and the *Cannington Herald*:

A London citizen who had recently hoped to become heir to a considerable Yorkshire estate is understood to have committed suicide at his home in Tooting just before the New Year. Police have ruled out foul play. It seems that the estate eventually went to a distant cousin who took precedence and that the disappointment at a time of pecuniary embarrassment was more than he could bear. We refer to Mr John Goode, of Graham Mansions, Gilmore Road. He is understood to have died intestate.

Police have closed the case of Mr Martin Gee, whose body was found on the Cannington Road, Halton Thoresby, on Christmas Day. Our readers will remember the sadness with which we announced his decease in our issue of 28 December. The coroner brought in a verdict of death by hypothermia after the deceased had ingested a home-prepared heart drug without regard for the physiological realities, and the police are now satisfied that no other party was involved. However, they have drawn our attention to a curious clause in his will. His estate is divided equally between a niece and a person who assisted him in the acquisition of an unexpected inheritance: 'that person will know to come forward in the event of my death'. Anyone who thinks he or she may qualify is asked to contact Messrs Boothby, Gilroy and Saddle by phoning London 773 4568 in office hours and quoting ref.23G/BS within 21 days of this intimation.

Would this flush out the accomplice and give enough leverage for a confession?

The inspector dreamed on. The premises of Messrs Boothby, Gilroy and Saddle (the name had popped unbidden into his subconscious) were, he imagined, situated up a flight of stone steps on the first floor of a building in the City. The entrance off the street was not prepossessing, and first impressions were unfavorable. However, the reception area and waiting-room were unexceptionable, and clients and inquirers were received in efficient fashion by the full-time receptionist, a certain Miss Amanda Wilson. Miss Wilson was forbidding at first sight, because her hair-style was severe and her eyes looked at you unflinchingly from behind heavy tortoiseshell spectacles. Her tight skirt brought her figure in. Part of her job being, as she saw it, to preserve the partners from the attentions of undesirables, she operated a system of filtering which disconcerted those not serious or confident in their search for legal expertise. To those, however, whom she weighed and found not wanting, she was courtesy personified.

The first person to call in answer to the advertisement placed so artfully in the *Cannington Herald* was a woman of middle-age, well-turned-out but not flashy, clearly nervous. Miss Wilson was quite aware that the advertisement would cause to crawl forth from the woodwork the hopeful, the avaricious, the scheming, the desperate–in short, a sad parade of deluded people, with the single exception of the right person, whoever that should turn out to be. She was, of course, right. The question was, into which category fitted the female personage standing before her now?

'Good morning, how may I help?'

'Well, I phoned two days ago to make an appointment. It's in answer to the advertisement, you see.'

'Oh, yes, I remember. You mean the advertisement in the *Cannington Herald*. You must be'–consulting her appointments' list–'Mrs Esme Crantock, am I right?'

'Yes, that's right.'

'Now Mrs Crantock, I hope you understand that Mr Saddle wishes to interview *bona fide* inquirers only. He has therefore asked me to submit a question to you, in writing. If you answer the question correctly, he will be happy to see you. If, on the other hand, you give the wrong answer, he hopes you will understand if he declines to interview you further. Do I make myself clear?'

The caller's nervousness visibly increased.

'Yes, quite clear, thank you,' she managed to say.

Miss Wilson handed her an envelope.

'In this envelope, Mrs Crantock, is the question, and here is a pen. Please feel free to go into the waiting-room'–indicating a door on the other side of the reception area–'and take as much time as you please. When you are happy, you can seal the envelope and hand it back to me. You will get an answer in a few minutes. Is that all right?'

Mrs Crantock hesitated.

'Yes, thank you,' she said and disappeared into the waiting-room. Minutes passed. More minutes passed. Eventually the woman emerged into the reception area.

'I'm sorry, I think I've made a mistake in coming.'

She cast the envelope on Miss Wilson's desk and vanished.

'Ah, well,' thought Miss Wilson, 'that's saved a mite of time. Won't be long before the next hopeful turns up, though.' And so the days passed. Men and women, old and young, rich and poor, the overweening and the timid - a sorry troop. As Robert Ingersoll once observed, 'Hope is the only universal liar who never loses his reputation for veracity'. Wickfield mused on what impelled people to try their luck even when the omens were unfavorable. Of course, if people were sensible enough to reject all foolish belief in supernatural powers like Luck, Fortune and Chance, their lives would be more contented. Life, the world, the universe, are governed by an intelligent, supreme Spirit or not at all, he thought. That Spirit is not going to subject people to the aleatoric vagaries of Chance; and if there were no such Spirit, why search for meaning at all? Perhaps people were so caught up in their own tiny capsules that they could not see the wider picture: a gracious and benevolent Godhead balancing the most disparate forces in order to conjure good out of what can sometimes seem like chaos. They saw only what lay under their noses: a chance–that word again!–to win a fortune by lying, pretending, cheating and in some cases murdering, without regard for the Divine Providence which could serve them so much better if they submitted to it. In the present case, they would weigh up the pros and cons. They would have to travel up to London; perhaps buy a new suit or outfit, to impress the lawyer-boffin; invest time in the venture; risk ridicule at the end. But what if they were successful? Oh, joy, a half-share in an entire estate! That surely outweighed the disadvantages and perils.

Is it legitimate to believe in Fate? The ancients had believed whole-heartedly in supernatural forces which had in their power the life of everyone on earth. They sat there, manipulating events and circumstances, shuffling humans around like pieces on a chess-board, causing now disaster, now good fortune, and all at a whim, without rhyme or reason. There could be no understanding Fate and no gainsaying it. How could people otherwise so civilized have fallen for such trumpery philosophy? To believe in Fate was to reduce humans to puppets. Actually, he realized, that wasn't quite right. Heroism consisted in using Fate to shape one's future, in the sense that virtue and vice arose out of the human struggle to fit in with the machinations of the gods: we were free to react in a number of ways to circumstances. The Greeks and Romans were not entirely lost in fatalism! Perhaps the callers at the offices of Boothby, Gilroy and Saddle reasoned that, if Fate was on their side and willed them to have the Gee estate, they couldn't lose. It did seem, however, a poor philosophy of life for any educated person in this day and age.

As he reasoned thus, the dream obtruded itself again. A woman in her late thirties (judged the redoubtable Miss Wilson) arrived, according to a previous telephone appointment, in response to the *Cannington Herald* advertisement.

'Good morning, my name is Heather Houseman. I phoned yesterday to make an appointment.'

'Yes, Mrs Houseman. I have you down here. You are welcome to the offices of Boothby Gilroy and Saddle, and Mr Saddle is looking forward to seeing you. But he wondered first whether you would be kind enough to answer one question, just to establish your *bona fides*. Please take this envelope and pen into the waiting-room, answer the question at your leisure, seal the envelope and bring it back to me. We can take matters from there.'

When Mrs Houseman opened the envelope, she found a single sheet of A4 paper. Half-way down it, neatly typed in capital letters, was the following question: 'What was Mr Martin Gee's original surname?' The question did not faze her, but she sat there wondering whether it was safe to admit knowledge of the answer. To give the correct answer would surely reveal to the lawyer that she knew of John Goode, of his plan to prise the Goode estate out of the Hotham grasp, and that Martin Gee was an obstacle to his ambitions. None of that, however, was illegal knowledge. If she were interviewed by Mr Saddle, could she safely admit, on the other hand, her role in tipping Goode off as to the Matthewson holiday? She didn't see why not. She could deny all knowledge of Dismore's murder of Gee. She could deny all knowledge of Goode's death except what was public knowledge through a national newspaper. Deciding to risk it, she wrote below the typed question a single word: 'Goode' and handed the sealed envelope back to Miss Amanda Wilson. Five minutes later, Miss Wilson said, 'Mr Saddle will see you now, Mrs Houseman'.

Mr Saddle was a dour, pinched individual, close to retirement to judge from his sallow features lined with crow's-feet and ringed by graying hair and beard. However, his manner was irreproachable.

'Mrs Houseman,' he began, 'do sit down. I trust we can conclude this interview to the entire satisfaction of my principal– if I may so refer to a will - and yourself. My only duty is to satisfy myself that you were instrumental in helping the late Mr Gee to the possession of the estates he did not live long enough, alas, to enjoy. His will is quite specific that half of the estate is to go to the person who helped him materially in this matter.'

'Yes,' said Mrs Houseman, 'that is why I am here.'

'Mrs Houseman,' continued the lawyer, 'on the phone you gave your address as 4, Torbay Villas, Cannington. Have I got that right?'

'Yes, quite right, Mr Saddle.'

'Good. Perhaps you'd be kind enough now just to outline the sequence of events leading up to Mr Gee's acquisition of the estate. To satisfy me, you will need, of course, to divulge information to which only the right person can be privy. I'm sure you understand that. Remember that I know the answers already.'

I wonder whether you do, thought his client.

'I can be brief, Mr Saddle, because, truth to tell, I did very little. An old university friend of mine wrote to me last year, saying that he wished to meet a distant cousin of his who lived near me but was afraid of his reception after a family feud. Could I help engineer a meeting? My friend was anxious to meet this cousin unannounced and incognito, so that he could satisfy himself as to his likely reception. So I told him how he could get to know a local family, without arousing any suspicions, who knew this distant cousin. The rest would be up to my friend. And that's all I did.'

'Well, now, Mrs Houseman, you are very clear so far, but you haven't quite satisfied me, I'm afraid. How did what you have told me benefit Mr Gee in the acquisition of the estate? That is the question before us, you know.'

'Well, my friend told me that he was expecting to come into a handsome estate in Yorkshire, through a family connection who had no issue, and that this other person would prefer to divide it between Mr Gee and my friend if the former were interested: but he was not going to entrust it to someone who had no interest, and it had to be someone with the surname Goode. My friend undertook to speak to Mr Gee on behalf of this family connection, with the greatest discretion, and to ascertain his, Mr Gee's, intentions.'

She paused.

'Yes, Mrs Houseman.' Mrs Houseman was wondering how far she could go in her story. She thought a little glossing was in order.

'In due course, I heard from my friend again that Mr Gee had agreed to inheriting half of the estate, and to changing his name back to Goode, which was apparently the original form of his surname. This was to ensure continuity of possession. The next thing I hear is that Mr Gee is found dead after an unfortunate confusion with a sleeping-tablet.'

'Please continue, Mrs Houseman.'

'When I saw your advertisement, I was very surprised, because I couldn't understand how my friend could consult with Mr Gee at Christmas and report back to the family benefactor and still leave time for Mr Gee to draw up his will by Christmas morning. It didn't seem to hang together.'

'So what did you conclude?'

'I thought the benefactor must have changed his mind and handed the whole estate over to Martin Gee, well before Christmas. Martin Gee then makes his will, leaving half to his niece–I never knew he had one–and half to the person who helped him, meaning my friend. Unfortunately, his wishes could never be fulfilled, because Fate intervened.'

'Fate? In what way?'

'My friend reports back to his principal, on Christmas Day or thereabouts, that unfortunately Mr Gee is dead. At that point the principal tells him that the estate had already been given to Gee, and that its future therefore rested with the wording of Gee's will. My friend had been cut out. He is so incensed, or grieved, or disappointed, that he takes his own life.'

'Yes, I see, but that would mean that Mr Gee knew already about your friend and his mediation between him, that is, Mr Gee, and the benefactor.'

'Oh, he did, I imagine, but he had no inkling at that stage that my friend was planning to visit him. All he knew was that the benefactor had got to hear of him via my friend, and he wished to demonstrate suitable gratitude.'

'In that case, Mrs Houseman, I don't see how you hope to benefit from the advertisement, because Mr Gee could not, at the time of making his will, have known about your role in this affair. You have acknowledged yourself that the "person who assisted him in the acquisition of an unexpected inheritance" was not you but your friend.'

'It is true that I did not help Mr Gee directly to his gift, but I eased the path for my friend, who was assisting Mr Gee to his windfall, and now that he is dead, I step in to claim his share of the estate, as he would have wished.'

'Thank you so much, Mrs Houseman. I have two further questions for you, if you will permit. Where does Mr Thornton Dismore come into all this?'

'Dismore was the name my friend opted to go under at Halton Thoresby. I thought it was silly, all this secrecy stuff, but he said it was necessary. And your second question?'

'May I ask how you hoped to benefit from the assistance afforded your friend, in the first instance?'

'I'm sorry, Mr Saddle, I don't see how this is relevant to the question at issue. You won't mind, I'm sure, if I decline to answer.'

'Well, Mrs Houseman, you have certainly satisfied me, I am glad to say, that you are the person I am looking for. But I am not absolutely certain that all is at it seems, and I hope you will give me a little time to mull things over. May I get in touch with you in Cannington in a few weeks?'

'That won't be possible, I'm afraid, as I'm going abroad for an extended visit connected with my work. May *I* contact *you* when I return? It may be some months.'

'Very well, Mrs Houseman, that will be acceptable.'

Mr Saddle ruminated. He hoped he had asked the woman the right questions to get her to incriminate herself. She had admitted knowing that Dismore was Goode in disguise. But she had admitted no knowledge of Goode's real intentions with regard to Gee or that she thought Goode had been in any way instrumental in Gee's death. Perhaps it was too much to expect her to admit these things. In any case, she had made out a plausible explanation of her own thinking. And what if she were right? Perhaps Detective Inspector Wickfield could shed some light on this mysterious affair.

As the inspector realized, however, when he snapped out of his reverie, a sting like that would not have worked anyway, even if it had been legal. A pity. It had, however, helped him to think round that side of the problem, and there was nothing wrong in dreaming that the forces of law and order were united in the defeat of evil. Now, however, he had to grapple with realities again, and he therefore turned his attention to the possibility of Nicholas Hotham's being the murderer of John Goode.

He, Wickfield, had returned to London three days before, after interviewing Hotham in his Roman palazzo. Appearances were against his host. Hotham was in London at the time, he had every motive; he might have had the means. The only way to find out was to return to the Hothams', and Wickfield persuaded himself that the gravity of the crime justified another trip to Rome. He decided not to inform the Hothams first either about Goode's murder or about his own impending visit. A lack of forewarning might not come amiss. With the girls back at school, it was highly unlikely that the parents had gone away. This time, knowing that the Gravina palace was centrally placed, he armed himself with a map and walked down from Termini station, enjoying the sensation of the busy Roman streets, even if the Via Nazionale was a long haul and Piazza Venezia an almost intolerable cacophony. He was readily admitted to the palazzo and made welcome. 'What a pleasant surprise! This must mean that you have made progress with our case,' and so on. Coffee was soon prepared in the *salone*.

During the short interval as refreshment was prepared, Wickfield asked himself whether pleasant surroundings outside one's school buildings made any difference to the quality of one's learning. Wickfield thought it must do. To be so stimulated and aesthetically fed twice a day to and from school, and to return at the end of the school day to an elegant if slightly run-down Roman palazzo, must have an uplifting effect, even though beauty seemed to register so little with some young people. Pop music? So ugly! Did youngsters not recognize ugliness when they heard it?

'Mr Hotham,' he began at length, when he and his hosts were settled, 'when I was last here, on 30 and 31 January, you had not long come back from visiting Mr Goode at his London flat. On 2 January we discovered his body and have launched a murder investigation.'

There were audible gasps from his hosts.

'I cannot conceal from you, and you must yourself fully realize, that you are a prime suspect. The pathologist calculates that Goode had been dead four or five days before his body was discovered. That places you perilously close to the time of his death, so I wonder whether you would be so kind as to run over again the events of 28 December.'

Hotham paused before speaking.

'Inspector, I realize that things don't look too good, if they stand as you have outlined them, but I swear to you that I had nothing to do with Goode's death, although heaven knows I didn't wish him well. Let me tell you, then, what happened on that day, although most of it you know already. I caught the 14.30 plane from Fiumicino, landed at Heathrow at 15.30 local time, or thereabouts, took the bus into central London, reached Goode's flat at approximately a quarter to six. We talked for an hour. And you know already exactly how the conversation went. He refused all offers to negotiate, insisted on his right to three-quarters of the estate and left me no choice but to accept his terms. I came away crushed. After that dreadful interview, I wandered into a pub–the Golden Goose in Heffer Street, I think it was, if you wish to check up–had a bit of refreshment, and then found a small hotel in a side-street. It was the, let me think, the Honeycomb Hotel, can't remember the name of the street. I've probably still got the bill in my suitcase, if you're interested. The next morning I made my way back to Heathrow and caught the first available plane home. I can assure you that when I left Goode on the evening of 28 December, he was alive and kicking–that is to say, he was alive and I was kicking'–he managed a rueful smile.

'According to the autopsy, Mr Hotham–and Mrs Hotham, of course–John Goode died during the evening of 28 December. The murderer had set up the body to appear as a suicide, but the pathologist was not of course deceived. By your own admission, you were in Goode's flat on the evening of his murder. Would you care to comment?'

Before he could speak, however, Mrs Hotham jumped in. '*Caro, non è vero: dimmi che non è vero!*' [Darling, it's not true: tell me it's not true!] Hotham reached for her hand and patted it gently.

'Inspector, I should be very foolish to bring about Goode's death. The papers in his flat would make it as plain as daylight that he was angling for the Hotham estates, and his death would automatically be attributed to me, particularly as my movements could so easily be checked. No, Inspector, killing Goode would put the noose round my own neck–figuratively speaking–and that would be a far crueller blow to my family than losing a quarter of the estate. But I didn't know then that no accommodation with him was possible: I had every hope he would be more merciful. You seem to be suggesting that I went to his flat with the specific intention of committing murder, but I've already explained that that would be suicidal. You've got to believe me, Inspector.'

The inspector was inclined to believe him.

'What caused his death, Inspector, if I may ask?'

'Poisoned: small dose of *oenanthe crocata*–dropwort to you and me, Mr Hotham.'

'But I've never even heard of it! What is it: some rare plant from the forests of the Amazon?'

'No, Sir, it's a common British wild flower that grows in ditches and wet spots in the south of England–and elsewhere in Europe, of course.'

'And how would I get hold of any of that, in central Rome?' The incredulity in his voice was either genuine or the work of a well-coached actor. 'If I had murdered him, it would have been on the spur of the moment, with an act of irresistible violence!'

'Mr Hotham, I accept your protestations of innocence, but if you don't mind, I must ask you to surrender your passport to the local police for the time being, and not to leave Rome without letting me know. Is that clear?'

XVI

The confidence of reason give,
And in the light of truth thy bondman let me live.
William Wordsworth, Ode to Duty, Stanza 7, lines 55-56

'Right, Sunshine,' said Wickfield to his sergeant, 'it's time you and I sat down and went over the whole business together. At the back of my mind is something we've been told that holds the key, but I can't for the life of me remember what it is. I'm hoping it will come back to me as we talk.'

They sat in the inspector's office. The windows were closed against the January day; a gas fire burned in the hearth. Coffee-cups and note-books were to hand for the crucial conference. Detective Inspector Wickfield speculated on the relationship of fact and theory. He had read somewhere that there is no such thing as a fact: all our knowledge is filtered through a sophisticated net of previous knowledge which sorts our incoming information into categories in order to make sense of it, so that facts–raw, unadulterated realities–are processed and manipulated before they ever reach our consciousness. That might be an interesting philosophical debate. As a policeman, however, he had to recognize and differentiate established data and more or less plausible theory. The data lay in the realm of forensic science: fingerprinting, X-rays, microscopic examination of fibres, and so forth. In the words of the illustrious Alexander Pope, 'What can we reason but from what we know?' The theory lay in the mind of the detective and depended on such imponderables as training, flair, experience, insight and, in no small measure, sheer bloody-mindedness. In the present case, there seemed to be a lot of data but no workable thread taking it all into account.

'This is it. We've got to crack this case, my lad, or I shall go nuts. Let's first of all put down the FACTS, what we *know* to be the case. Then we can pencil in the various hypotheses that cover the facts: our guesswork, if you like. Here, take some paper. Let's arrange our facts not in order of discovery but in order of occurrence.

1. The Hothams in Rome receive the first intimation of impending disaster: a letter from John Goode dated 11 December and posted in London.
2. Hotham's first visit to Goode in London, 15 December.
3. The death of Martin Gee. Body found 25 December; digoxin taken during the hour and a half previous to 1 a.m.
4. Constable Pudden's initiation of local inquiries at Halton Thoresby, 25 December. CID called in 26 December. The existence of Matthewson's first marriage is revealed by a newspaper cutting in Gee's house.
5. CID's first local inquiries: six villagers have reason to hate Gee, 27 December.
6. Hotham's second visit to Goode in London, 28 December. Goode dies.
7. Wickfield's inspection of Dismore's London flat and questioning of the Matthewsons about their Christmas guest, 28 December.
8. Spooner's call on Gee's niece in Coventry: she and her husband are revealed to have a motive for murder, 29 December.
9. Wickfield's first visit to the Hothams in Rome, 30-31 December.
10. Probable identification of Goode and Dismore, 31 December.
11. Discovery of Goode's body, five days dead, 2 January a.m.

12. Goode's membership of F3P6 discovered in a search of Goode's flat, 2 January p.m.
13. Provisional identification of Goode's Halton Thoresby accomplice, 3 January.
14. Wickfield's interviews with members of John Goode's Ipswich family: mother, sister and aunt, 4 January.
15. Spooner's interview with "Mr Smith" of F3P6 in London, 4 January.
16. Wickfield's second visit to Rome to interview Nicholas Hotham, 6 January.

'Let's also list briefly what each interview has yielded in terms of information. We can also take these in chronological order. Somewhere here, I'm convinced, lies the key to the mystery.

Mr Vickers. Gee was not given to drink. Linford had a grudge against Gee because of a mistaken bid at auction. Wife not interviewed on this occasion.

Dr and Mrs Simpson. Nothing noteworthy in Gee's behavior. Gee had denounced the doctor to the GMC.

Mr Matthewson. Admitted his present marriage was bigamous, but had no idea how Gee had found out or indeed that he had found out. Mrs Matthewson not present.

Mr and Mrs Linford. The pair admitted their grudge against Gee over the painting. They let slip that Mrs Vickers had been rebuffed by Gee on a little sexual advance.

Mr Thew. Admitted to a prejudice against homosexuals.

Mr Gee's bank-manager. No surprises. Gee's account in funds.

Mr Gee's solicitor. Gee's will leaves most of his property to a niece.

Mrs Vickers. Admitted to disliking Gee because he had rebuffed her.

Mrs Matthewson. Gave them Dismore's London address.

Mr and Mrs Matthewson again. Revealed Mr Dismore's ploy to inveigle an invitation to Halton Thoresby for Christmas.

Mr and Mrs Tucker. Denied all knowledge of the contents of Uncle Martin's will, but a need of money became apparent.

Mr and Mrs Hotham. No previous knowledge of Goode. His revelations a complete surprise to them.

Mrs Goode. History of John Goode from a mother's perspective.

Mrs Seacroft. Confirmed Goode's passion for genealogy.

Miss Goode. Confirmed Mrs Seacroft's information above.

Mr Smith alias *Graf Otto.* F3P6 would not on any account get involved in illegal activities.

'Now, those are acquisitions of knowledge, things to work on. We cannot doubt that there is some connection between the Hotham business in Rome, based on Joan Goode's will, and the death of Mr Gee in Halton Thoresby. Two things lead us to this conclusion: Goode disguises himself as Thornton Dismore and puts in an appearance at Halton Thoresby on the day Gee dies; and Gee is revealed to be a Goode with some right, apparently, to inherit or take over Hotham's Yorkshire estates.

'Sergeant, just run through the most likely hypotheses, will you?'

'Right, Sir. Hypothesis No.1. Gee is not murdered at all but dies through misadventure. John Goode is murdered by Nicholas Hotham to prevent the implementation of his plan to deprive the Hothams of their inheritance.

Hypothesis No.2. Gee is murdered by one of the inhabitants of Halton Thoresby, for any one of a number of reasons. John Goode's murder as above.

Hypothesis No.3. Gee is murdered by Goode, for which he needs an accomplice resident on site. This accomplice turns on Goode and murders him in his London flat. Hotham is innocent of any crime.

Hypothesis No.4. Gee is murdered by his niece, who needs the money. Goode is murdered by an agent of F3P6 for sinning against the organization's rules.

Hypothesis No.5. Gee is murdered by a local. The fact becomes known to John Goode, perhaps in his character as Thornton Dismore. Goode decides on a little blackmail and is murdered to prevent further threats.

Hypothesis No.6. None of the above. Gee's death is an accident, Goode is done to death by an unknown assailant for reasons as yet undiscovered: perhaps he had defrauded his grocer.'

'There's no need to be flippant, Spooner. We're in enough difficulty without your making jokes about it.'

'Sorry, Sir, slip of the tongue. Well, to continue. We can't really prove any of these suggestions. In any case, the truth may be a combination of several of them, in whole or in part. For example, hypotheses 1 and 2 are not mutually exclusive. So where do we go from here?'

'We look at them all carefully, weighing the weaknesses and the strengths. Let's work our way through them.

'No.1. The post mortem on Gee was inconclusive, so he could well have died through misadventure: he took the drug himself during the midnight service without due appreciation of its action. But I can't really see Hotham as the murderer of Goode. As he says, he had no reason to think that Goode couldn't be persuaded to soften his demands, and yet the use of a syringe seems to suggest premeditation. On the other hand, he was on the spot at more or less the crucial time, and he had every motive.

'No.2. We have seen that at least seven of the Halton Thoresby inhabitants had reason to desire Gee's removal. They all had opportunity. What worries me, however, is that none of their motives seems sufficiently weighty to lead to murder. And is any of them sufficiently ruthless? Perhaps.

'No.3. Now here we seem to be on more plausible ground. Let us work on the understanding that Goode's accomplice is Roberta Linford. She is an old university friend of Goode's. We know he had an unfortunate love-affair at university, which turned him in on himself and made him unable to approach females thereafter, but there is nothing to suggest that he had renounced female friendships already made. In any case, Roberta Linford was not a close friend, let us say, but an acquaintance with whom Goode kept loosely in touch. He contacts her, promises her a handsome honorarium in return for a little help in a business transaction of his–the less he reveals of its nature the better–and then for some reason reneges on his promise. She, fearing disclosure of her part in the "transaction", if she suspected that the murder of Gee was part of it, or furious at Goode's refusal to pay her as promised, runs up to London and does away with him. That lets Hotham off the hook and makes F3P6 a red herring. Can we prove that Mrs Linford made a trip to London on 28 December and murdered Goode? Not easily, if at all. Let's move on.

'No.4. The weakness here, if weakness it is, is that the two crime scenes have no connection with each other. It is possible, but I should say unlikely. The greatest argument against it is that I just don't see how Mrs Tucker and her husband Bill could have murdered Gee. Also, she professed to be quite ignorant of inheriting from her uncle in case of his death, although of course that may be bluff. It doesn't explain why Goode adopted a pseudonym and involved an accomplice at Halton Thoresby. No, I am inclined to reject hypothesis no.4 outright.

'No.5. When we suggest that Gee was murdered by "a local", do we mean Mrs Linford? Not necessarily, I suppose. How does Dismore discover the crime? Did he see the perpetrator slip some tincture of digitalis into Gee's glass? That's possible. But why was Goode at Halton Thoresby, disguised as Dismore? Perhaps Goode was trying to discover whether Gee had any knowledge of his ancestry or interest in the Hotham/Goode estates. To arrive openly as Goode might alert Gee to the possibilities of possession of an estate if he had any inkling of the origin of his surname. His visit was a reconnaissance, not very noble but not criminal either. So Goode sees the concoction of the potion that killed Gee, phones up or speaks *viva voce* to the murderer and threatens revelation. On Christmas Day morning, he hears of Gee's death, comes across a rumour, unwittingly circulated by Constable Pudden, that all might not be above board, puts two and two together and makes out of the sum a motive to coin a little money on the side. But can we prove it?

'As for No.6, while we can't rule it out of court, I'd be very surprised if none of the motives and opportunities our inquiries have uncovered had any bearing on Goode's activities or death.

'In any case, I still feel that the answer is staring us in the face, and yet I cannot put my finger on it. Let's think about it for a while and return after lunch. I've promised to meet my missus at The Red Hart, and I might be better equipped to cope with this investigation after a little refreshment. Shall we say back here at 2?'

The inspector strode purposefully over to The Red Hart. His wife was already ensconced in an alcove, back to the wall on a plush leather settee, nose in a newspaper. Beth was a homely, handsome woman: thick black hair, dark brown eyes, several chins, a smile permanently playing round her lips, medium height and build, perhaps tending to portly, a woman any man might be proud of as wife and mother of his sons. In character, she was far distant from her husband. Where he was an avid absorber of culture, she preferred the glossy magazines kind patients left for the waiting-room of the medical practice where she worked as a receptionist; where he was a thinker, indeed a philosopher, she was a doer, impatient of what she regarded as futile speculation. 'Never gets you anywhere', she would say, with some pretension to accuracy. 'Put all the world's philosophers together for a week, and you still wouldn't get a sensible answer.' Her common sense was what had given her husband anchorage in reality for all these years. And perhaps her greatest virtue in her husband's eyes was that she never wittered. Theirs was a marriage blessed by contentment and mutual warmth.

They had met in inauspicious circumstances. Stan Wickfield was collecting back the envelopes he had delivered the previous week round an estate in Birmingham, on behalf of a local charity run by the Church of St Saviour's; he hoped they were plump with notes, or at least coinage. It was, he remembered fondly, a Friday evening, when folks were likely to be in even if they went out later. It was pouring with rain. He was on the last few houses of his round and looking forward to trotting home himself, when a young woman with large brown eyes and a bewitching smile opened the door to his knock. In response to his request for the envelope, instead of reaching for it, she said, 'You poor man, come on in out of the rain for a few minutes and have a cup of tea with us'. She ushered him, without waiting for his response, into a small living-room where her parents were sitting on a sofa in front of the fire. The room was comfortably furnished and above all welcoming. As he stood at the front door half an hour later to take his leave of the young woman, he said, apprehensively, 'You wouldn't like a supper out one day next week, would you–that is,' he added hastily–'if you're not attached?' 'I'd love to,' she said, and that was the start of a life-time's romance.

He was then at police college. After steady achievements at grammar school and good A-Levels in English, Religious Studies and (of all things!) Latin, he could not decide what to do with himself. His father was a doctor in general practice, but medicine was not for him. No one in his family had a police background, but he thought that policing was a way of helping society that was within his capabilities. So off to police college he went. And now, at the age of fifty-two, he was a detective inspector and more than happy with his lot.

He approached his wife, kissed her on the forehead and asked, 'What's that you're reading?' He sat down beside her. 'I've ordered for you,' she said. 'Mushroom pie and chips. Will that do? I'm having a tuna salad.

'It's a paragraph about a case that's racking Italy at the moment. Here, listen to this:

The bare facts (if our gentle readers will pardon the phrase) are as follows. On 8 July 1972, a young couple, whose names cannot be released for legal reasons, married in Pesaro. Relatives and friends attended the usual banquet, and the auspices for a happy married life were favorable. To the family's horror, the young husband, aged twenty-three, announced white-faced the following morning that his bride was not a virgin as she had led him to believe and that he was therefore seeking an annulment of the marriage. The court has just pronounced sentence [eighteen months later! interjected Beth]. Under article 180 of the civil code, a marriage can be annulled 'if there is an error … concerning the essential qualities of the person'. The article does not enumerate the 'essential qualities', but the judges decided that virginity was one of them.

'And the article goes on to report the outrage from feminist groups and others and the heated debate rocking Italy at this time. Apparently the whole event is a cauldron of religious, political and social susceptibilities, so it looks set to ferment for a while.'

'And which side are you on, my dear?' asked Wickfield.

'Well, I don't know yet, not until I've read the arguments on both sides. Probably a storm in a tea-cup: these things usually are. I'll let you know when I've made up my mind. In the meantime, get on with your pie!'

'I've never understood why the Christian church has prized virginity so much. Books, I daresay whole libraries, have been written in praise of virginity as a way to God, while marriage is only for those not strong enough to withstand the temptations of the flesh, a poor second best. How do the clergy expect the church to flourish? In any case, that attitude demeans the heroic efforts of married people who try to live by the Christian code. There seems little doubt that Jesus himself was married, and what's good enough for Jesus is good enough for me!'

'How do you know Jesus was married? We're always being told he was celibate–and that's why priests are celibate.'

'*Some* priests: only Roman ones. The rest have seen the light. Jesus was married because all Jews got married: there was just no tradition of celibacy. Do you know, in the whole 2000 years of Jewish history in the Old Testament, there is only one celibate.'

'Who?'

'The prophet Jeremiah. But we're not sure even about him, as the text doesn't necessarily mean physical celibacy for life. And my second reason for saying Jesus was married is that he didn't appear in public life, we're told, until he was "about thirty"–plenty of time to get married, have a family and be widowed. What's the matter with that? In other words, why wait until you're thirty, unless you have family ties?'

'A proper little theologian, aren't we?'

'One advantage of celibacy, I suppose, is that one is not propelling unwilling offspring into life in the twentieth century, even though someone's got to do it. I sometimes wonder how the human race survives at all,' he continued between munches. 'So many families seem to lurch from crisis to crisis. So many factors–bereavement, war, social upheavals, ignorance, stupidity, negligence, illness, you name it–threaten to destroy the stability of the building-block of society, it's amazing where the kids' resilience comes from that enables them to be parents in their turn.'

'Well, Stan, part of your answer lies in the Holy Book you go on about. Just look how God picked and chose amongst members of the same families: Abel but not Cain, Isaac but not Ishmael, Jacob but not Esau, and so on. It's Providence interfering in the growth of family life that enables the human race to continue by steering it to happy outcomes. Dearie me, I'm getting as bad as you, now, warbling on about fanciful things.'

Her husband, however, was no longer listening. A look of complete absorption suffused his features. He had ceased to munch, almost to breathe. He sat there taking stock of a brilliant insight. Eventually he was all motion.

'That's it!' he shouted. 'That's the answer! You've done it, my dear!' With that, he left his meal unfinished, kissed her hastily on the forehead and ran back to the station, the case of Joan Goode's will solved at last.

XVII

Attempt the end, and never stand to doubt;
Nothing's so hard but search will find it out.

Robert Herrick, Seek and Find

'Right, Sergeant,' said Wickfield, handing him a sheet of paper, 'I want these three people brought in for questioning, please. You can tell them they're arrested on suspicion of being an accessory to murder, murder, and conspiracy to murder. We'll see whether they all stand by each other when the moment of truth comes.'

It was Disraeli who said, if he remembered correctly, 'Assassination has never changed the history of the world', but was Disraeli right? So many prominent figures had been assassinated, it was difficult to believe that the course of history had *never* been altered by it. Martin Luther King? Thomas à Becket? Julius Caesar? And if Hitler, for example, had been the victim of one of the plots against him, say in 1941, would not the war have had a different outcome? Of course, the what-ifs of history were notoriously difficult to assess. The fact remained that history was, as Gibbon knew, 'little more than the register of the crimes, follies and misfortunes of mankind'. What made people take that fatal step of depriving somebody else of their right to life? He supposed almost as many reasons as there were murderers: greed, desperation, envy, guilt, self-aggrandizement, lack of self-control and so on. Did his job in any way right the balance? He hoped so. Of course, many deaths were brought about whose perpetrators were never brought to justice, but that was not a reason not to try either to prevent murder or, as in the present case, to catch up with those responsible for murder. And yet, when all was said and done, murder would continue–and genocide, and war, and violence, and rape, and terror. What a sorry lot the human race were! Roll on retirement, when he could decline into a peaceful old age and forget the follies and crimes of his fellow-humans!

Mrs Roberta Linford was the first to be questioned. Thirty-eight years old, in a position of educational responsibility, a well-educated woman with status in her local society, healthy pursuits and constructive pastimes. He hazarded that it was a gambling debt she was so anxious to settle that had misled her into crime, and he turned out to be right. There was a very fine line between behavior which is morally grey and behavior which is morally black, and the temptation to cross it often subtle and, to the lax conscience, imperceptible. Activities which are acceptable but of doubtful value can, with little encouragement, slip into downright immorality or illegality.

'Do sit down, Mrs Linford'–he was tempted to say 'Mrs Houseman' but thought that would be mischievous as well as unintelligible.

'Mrs Linford, there is a very serious charge to be made against you: accessory to murder, if not murder itself. We are going to deal with realities, not with façades and make-believe, so please concentrate, and above all be quite clear that I shall unearth the truth. The truth is just what we haven't had from you so far in this investigation. You told me the first time we met that you knew of no enemies that Mr Gee might have had. That wasn't true, was it?'

'Inspector, what I *suspected* was not to be trotted out as gospel, surely?'

'Perhaps it would be best, Mrs Linford, if you now told me the whole story, from the beginning.'

Mrs Linford looked at him in a manner he found it difficult to interpret. Was she still wondering how much he knew and therefore how much she could get away with?

'Some months ago, early last summer, I had a surprise letter from John Goode. We knew each other quite well at Durham, where we were both doing Modern Languages. It had never got beyond friendship, but we kept up over the years with a Christmas card or the occasional postcard from a holiday resort. We met once or twice in London. Otherwise I never expected to hear from him. In this letter, he said he had traced a distant cousin of his to Halton Thoresby and was anxious to look him up on family business. Unfortunately, because there had been a family row, John was uncertain how he would be received and therefore wanted to make the first contact incognito. He said that, since he and this cousin hadn't met for years, there was little likelihood that the cousin would recognize him facially.'

'Yes?'

'So I set up a little scheme for him. He was to pretend to meet by accident a couple of villagers who were holidaying in Cyprus, the Matthewsons, and through them, if he played his cards right, he would receive an invitation to stay at Halton Thoresby for a couple of days at Christmas. And that was it.'

'Mrs Linford, I have warned you, please: I want the whole truth. Your little plan seems very elaborate just for a meeting between cousins. Did John Goode tell you anything about the "family business"?'

'Apparently it had to do with a family estate which the then owner was anxious to offload on to John and this cousin, Martin Gee. The only stipulation was that both should adopt the permanent surname of Goode and agree to use the arms– although in this day and age that doesn't count for much. On the other hand, a nice bit of crested notepaper could impress your stock-broker!'

'But you suspected that the visit did not bode well for Martin Gee?'

'I thought perhaps John had an ulterior purpose. The secrecy he insisted on was somehow threatening. It seemed more likely to me that Martin Gee was somehow to be excluded from the scheme than benefit from the offer of half a fortune, but I never dreamt of *murder*! Why should I? John had something of the night about him, but taking someone's life is altogether different.'

'What did you get out of helping Goode further his little plan?'

'Inspector, I shall be quite frank with you.'

About time, my lady, if I may say so. It's taking us a long time to get to the truth.

'I was hard up–a little foolish betting, and I couldn't let my husband know. John promised to clear my debt for me.'

'Did you help him in any other way when he was in Halton Thoresby?'

'Only by pretending never to have seen him before.'

'And then?' interjected the inspector after a pause.

'That's it. That's all.'

'No, Mrs Linford. That is not by any means all. On Christmas Day, as soon as you heard that Gee was dead, you phoned Goode in London to ask for your remuneration, as your creditor was getting impatient. Isn't that so?'

'Oh, Inspector,' was all she said in reply before bursting into tears. After a few moments in which to regain her composure, she resumed her narrative.

'Yes, I phoned him, and he said that we had never made a firm agreement, that the full sum I mentioned was out of the question, but that he was happy to give me £100 as a token of his gratitude for my help.'

'So you went up to London to have it out with him. And you murdered him!'

'No, no, Inspector, it wasn't at all like that, you've got to believe me. A few days after my phone-call, the 28 December it was, I did decide to go up to London. I'd never been to his flat before, but I'd always had his address since he'd moved in there, and he was not difficult to find. He said he was too busy to talk to me; he'd just got rid of another visitor, he said, and he had a lot to think about. But I wasn't to be put off. We had a row, I took my £100 and left, promising that he hadn't heard the last of it. When I left that flat, Inspector, John Goode was as alive as you and I are. I drove back to Halton Thoresby and told my husband

I'd been out to see my sister in Reading. That's all I know of the affair.'

'No, Mrs Linford, it's still not all you know of the affair. I want the rest, please.'

How much did this inspector know, for heavens' sake? He seemed to be omniscient. Or was it skillful guessing? A troubled look came over Mrs Linford's face. She twisted her hands. Tears again came to her eyes.

'Look, Mrs Linford, whatever your role in this business, the truth is always the best policy, you know.'

'You are right, of course, Inspector,' and she seemed to take hold of herself. 'Well, matters escalated. Just before Christmas I had a phone-call from John's family, saying that they had found my address and details of my help amongst the wodge of papers that John had given them and hoped I would help them too. All I had to do was to let them know if anything happened to Gee, and they would pay me for my trouble. That was all I had to do: phone to say, "Martin Gee is dead", if that is what should happen. Seemed easy money, so I went along with it.'

'If that is all, Mrs Linford, why are you so reluctant to tell me?'

'Because I guessed there was dirty work afoot, but I swear I never knew any more than what I've told you. I don't want to be thought to have anything to do with John's death!'

'Mrs Linford, I think I believe you, so that will do for the moment, but I warn you that we may not be finished. And if in the meantime anything more occurs to you, I advise you to tell me at once. Honesty is the best policy. And you wouldn't want to be done for Goode's murder, would you? You admit yourself you were in his flat on the night he died, and you certainly had motive enough.'

The next person to be interviewed was Marcus Goode, cousin to John. John's father James had a sister Alice and a younger brother David, although of the three siblings only Alice still lived. She had never married. She was now in her early seventies, so it was probably too late for her to consider the step. James had married and reared a family of three. David had married an admirable woman called Tracy Johnston, who worked in an aid agency, in 1934, and they had two sons, Marcus, born in 1936, and Nathan, born two years later. Marcus, now nearly forty, had been living with a female friend for years, but they had no family, had never got married and had no plans to do so. He worked as a middle manager for a retail firm in Ipswich.

He sauntered in, dressed in jeans and jumper; tall and well-built, close-cropped hair, a certain debonair manner about him, but a truculent tone from the start. 'Why have I been brought in like this? I know nothing about John's death. You can't keep me here.'

'Mr Goode, please calm down. We are looking for the truth, and that is all you need to tell us. When did you last see your cousin John?'

'Don't know. Last summer? Never saw very much of him: bit of a wimp, if you ask me, and we'd never really got on. Nathan's little girl was christened in the summer, and there was a bit of a family get-together.'

'Then how do you explain that you were seen coming out of his London flat on the night of 28 December last?'

Pause. Long pause.

'I didn't kill him! Who saw me leave his flat?'

'A neighbor was on the stair coming down as you came out. She described you to us, and there is no mistaking the accuracy of her description.'

'Yes, all right, I went to his flat. The door wasn't locked. When I went in, he was there at a table in the sitting-room, quite dead. He'd killed himself with a bottle of whisky and some tablets.'

'Why did you go to see him?'

'Look, Inspector, this is going to sound a bit far-fetched.'

'Try me, anyway.'

'I knew John had had some little scheme in his head for a while. Apparently he'd unearthed a will which showed that the Goodes should by rights be owners of lands in Yorkshire, and he was determined to make himself master of the estate. Always had ideas above his station, did our John. There was something in this will about the estate-owners having to have the surname

Goode, and the present owners weren't called Goode: Witham or Holtham, or something. The main obstacle to John's scheme was a distant cousin called Gee, and I think John had some idea about persuading Gee to renounce all claim to the estate. When I heard that Gee had, shall we say, met with an accident, I began to realize that John was serious about his scheme. So I thought I would call on him to share some of the proceeds with me as a reward for my telling no one what I knew–or guessed. Some nasty-minded people like you, Inspector, would call that blackmail, but I'd call it offering a helping hand to a family-member in a difficult situation.'

'So far, Mr Goode, I follow you, but I have to say I don't believe you. Let me put it to you this way. You quickly realized that, as John had discovered, if Gee were removed from the scene, cousin John would be able to forward his claim to the estate. By the same token, if John were removed from the scene, you could put forward a claim to the estate, because you would then be the senior male Goode living, in John's place. You hadn't done any of this research, but papers in John's flat would have made it abundantly clear to you. You didn't go up to London to blackmail John: you went up to murder him! By making it look like suicide, you thought no one would suspect you. The way was then clear for you to carry out John's scheme on your own account and "persuade" Nicholas Hotham to give you three-quarters of the estate. How am I doing?'

'I didn't kill him! I can't prove it, but you've got to believe me. He was already dead when I got to the flat!'

'You'd been revolving this scheme in your head for some time, maybe many months,' pursued the inspector. 'Like the rest of the family, you'd been intrigued by John's researches and by the hint of money and status–gentrification, we might call it. You came to know the extent of John's researches and the secret workings of his elaborate scheme. You saw no reason why John, whom you despised for his social ineptitude and envied for his position as senior to you in the family, should benefit from a windfall, at the expense of the rest of the family. You couldn't bear the thought of John a landed gentleman with a coat of arms and a centuries-old estate, perhaps a country mansion to go with it, while you stayed unchanged.'

'You can't prove I murdered him!' was all Marcus found to answer.

'So you say,' said the inspector drily. 'We'll leave it at that for the moment, Mr Goode, but I shall need to see you again.'

Now for the third interview. Miss Alice Goode looked as spruce as before, unfazed by being arrested on a charge of conspiracy to murder. A smart two-piece, recent hair-do, well manicured hands, confident manner–which was soon to evaporate, however, as Detective Inspector Wickfield exercised his notorious charm.

'Miss Goode, when you and I met last, on'–quick consultation of note-pad–'4 January, you withheld the truth from me. I want the truth now, please, without prevarication or concealment. Everything, you understand. From the beginning.'

Miss Goode's composure wavered. Her lip quivered.

'Inspector, this is very hard, you know. I'm a single woman. I've led a quiet and blameless life. I saw my way to a little excitement and a little glamour, and there's no harm in that, is there? We're all entitled to a bit of fun!'

'But not at the expense of someone's life, Miss Goode,' was the stern rejoinder. 'Please continue.'

'When John came to see me, in May of last year, as I told you, he unfolded a scheme he had in his mind to recover a large family estate that, with a bit of effort, could make us all rich. His researches had unearthed a blip in the system, and he had a fool-proof plan to right a grievous wrong. He just needed some money to complete his researches.

'When I'd put him on to F3P6, I got him to promise me to keep me abreast of his plans, because I was interested. Gradually, over the months, I got to hear about his meeting with the Matthewsons in Cyprus, then his contacts with the Hothams, then his visit to Halton Thoresby and finally Gee's death. That was an accident, he told me, nothing to do with him. It was just so lucky that the man he was keen to eliminate eliminated himself.'

'And that was when your thoughts turned to a little scheme of your own, am I right?'

'Yes. And I'm not proud of it, but it was a chance not to be missed. You see, I'd never liked John: a simpering, wimpish sort of lad with a very foolish mother. No good with the girls, couldn't get himself sorted, dead-end job. Marcus, on the other hand, was dynamic and outgoing and needed only a bit of money, I thought, to make a real go of things. John's papers had told me that he, John, was the only obstacle in Marcus' way to taking the estate for himself. So I put the matter to Marcus. What could we do? It was Marcus who came up with the plan to murder John.'

'Well, maybe, but I bet you sowed the seeds of the idea in his head.'

'What if I did? Only a bit of thinking aloud. No harm in that. But if the scheme was to work, Marcus had to get in between Gee's death, which left the way open to John, and John getting the estate off Hotham, in case he immediately made a will leaving it to a donkey-shelter or bird-sanctuary. Quite a narrow window, this might be, we didn't know. My information was that John had persuaded Hotham to cough up and that the legal side would be tied up as soon after Christmas as possible. So Marcus had to strike between hearing of Gee's death and any possible legal procedure in the transference of the estate to John. Marcus could then approach Hotham with exactly the same information about Joan Goode's will and about Hotham's private life that John was going to use as a lever on Hotham.'

'Sorry! what was that about Hotham's private life?'

'Oh, didn't you know? John found out in the course of his researches that Hotham had had an affair in the early days of his marriage and had fathered a child on a Finnish girl.'

Ah, Wickfield thought to himself: so I was right!

'And you primed Mrs Roberta Linford to let you know when Gee was dead,' Wickfield continued.

'Yes. I found her details in John's papers–but I already knew of her from what John was telling me about his plans. It was a simple matter to persuade her to help us out with a phone-call, on the understanding that if she didn't, her involvement in John's scheme of doing away with Gee would be quietly handed in to the police.'

'But didn't she realize that helping you in a second murder would be even worse?'

'Perhaps she did, but getting a second bribe on top of our threat proved very persuasive, Inspector. In any case, Marcus didn't resort to murder: as I've told you quite clearly, John was dead when Marcus got to his flat. It must've been that Linford woman, keen to get her hands on more of the money than was coming her way via John. What will happen now?'

'Miss Goode, this has been a very sorry story, and your part in it will ensure that you go down for a long while, I'm glad to say. For the moment, I shall need you to make a statement and sign it, and then eventually it will be up to the court to decide on who did what when. I hope in the meantime you can come to terms with your conscience. Whether nephew John was a murderer or not, encouraging Marcus to remove him is not the way respectable people go about things. Well, you'll have plenty of time to ponder these matters. And can I leave you with a little thought from our friend Isaac Watts?

Birds in their little nests agree;
And 'tis a shameful sight
When children of one family
Fall out, and chide, and fight.

'Goodbye, Miss Goode.'

Later that afternoon, Wickfield and Spooner were running over the case. Spooner asked Inspector Wickfield why John Goode had pretended to them to be married with a family.

'Wishful thinking, I imagine. Fancied himself a married man with a son to carry on the Goode name. Harmless, really, except that it shows how far his plans had taken hold of his imagination.'

He remembered an old crossword clue: 13 across. Degenerate weakling has no descendants (3,2,4). He had been annoyed at the time, he remembered, that the answer had not leaped to his mind.

'And my really important question is this, Sir. You said that something someone had said in the course of our investigation held the key to the whole affair but that you couldn't remember what it was. Can you tell me now?'

'Yes, my lad, I can, because my wife jogged my memory. When I was first interviewing Miss Goode in her Ipswich house, she let drop two things that only later came to my mind. Firstly, she revealed that she knew who Hotham was. She tried to cover it up, but by then it was too late. If she knew who Hotham was, the chances were that she was familiar with the whole of Goode's scheme. The second thing was that she despised John and much preferred his cousin Marcus. It was my wife who triggered off this memory with her mention of God taking a preference to one brother over another in the Old Testament. It immediately became clear to me that Aunt Alice had concocted a scheme of her own whereby her favorite nephew Marcus would benefit from the Hotham estates over her brother James' child. I had already come to the conclusion that the key to understanding Goode's death was the will, because that's where the high stakes were: money, and lots of it. I then went back to the family tree, because if the will was involved, so were the family. I noticed then, what I had not noticed before, that Marcus stood in the same relation to Goode as Goode himself did to Gee. It also seemed likely, given the relationship between the two cousins, that there was a go-between linking Marcus and John. '

'Amazing–Sir! So did Goode murder Gee, or was it an accident?'

'We shall probably never know, and I'm not sure it matters very much now. If Gee was murdered, it was 99% certainly through Goode's actions, since he of all our suspects had the strongest motive and a ruthless streak to boot. He's now having to explain his part to his Maker, and I am sure justice will be done without our interference.'

'And who murdered Goode? Was it Roberta Linford or Marcus Goode?'

'Oh, Marcus. Forgot to tell you we had a lab report in: they found traces of his saliva on the glass. He had used gloves to set up the suicide appearance. He emptied the poisoned glass and either rinsed it thoroughly or substituted a fresh one, but before putting in a new mixture of whisky and Manerix, to mislead the poor police, he took a swig of whisky, possibly to steady his nerves–and forgot to wipe the rim! Forensics is a wonderful science, Sergeant!'

Lightning Source UK Ltd.
Milton Keynes UK
28 November 2009

146869UK00001B/59/P